Setter UP

Setter UP

Caelan Beard

JAMES LORIMER & COMPANY LTD., PUBLISHERS
TORONTO

James Lorimer & Company Ltd., Publishers acknowledges funding support from the Ontario Arts Council (OAC), an agency of the Government of Ontario. We acknowledge the support of the Canada Council for the Arts. This project has been made possible in part by the Government of Canada and with the support of Ontario Creates.

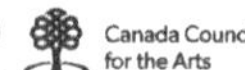

Cover design: Tyler Cleroux
Cover image: Shutterstock

Library and Archives Canada Cataloguing in Publication

Title: Setter up / Caelan Beard.
Names: Beard, Caelan, author.
Identifiers: Canadiana (print) 20250112108 | Canadiana (ebook) 20250112124 | ISBN 9781459419988 (hardcover) | ISBN 9781459419971 (softcover) | ISBN 9781459419995 (EPUB)
Subjects: LCGFT: Novels.
Classification: LCC PS8603.E244 S48 2025 | DDC jC813/.6—dc23

Published by:
James Lorimer & Company Ltd., Publishers
117 Peter Street, Suite 304
Toronto, ON, Canada
M5V 0M3
www.lorimer.ca

Distributed in Canada by:
Formac Lorimer Books
5502 Atlantic Street
Halifax, NS, Canada
B3H 1G4
www.formaclorimerbooks.ca

Distributed in the US by:
Lerner Publisher Services
241 1st Ave. N.
Minneapolis, MN, USA
55401
www.lernerbooks.com

Printed and bound in Canada.

To Agnes

CHAPTER ONE

Bouncing

"MACKENZIE — move!"

"GOT IT!" I yell, diving for the ball.

I get there just in time, bumping the volleyball to the teammate to my left, Soraya. She spikes it over the net, and the point is ours.

Our team lets out a small cheer, and Soraya, grinning, reaches down to help me up. I smile, taking her hand, but make sure I let go the second I'm up. I walk away, shaking it off, and get ready for the next rally. It's the last day of volleyball camp for the summer and I want to soak in every moment of my final game.

I love volleyball. I've played since grade seven, and for the last three years, I feel like most of my life has been about this sport: my schedule rotating around games, practices before and after school, and weekends spent hanging out with my teammates.

Last year, in grade nine, I made the varsity junior girls' volleyball team at school. The junior team is for grades nine and ten, but they don't take a lot of grade nine players, so it was a big deal. And I was so excited. I love everything about the game, and just stepping on court gives me a thrill, every damn time.

Then last year, in the middle of the school year and volleyball season, I came out as queer. It wasn't a big deal — I didn't have a big announcement, I sort of just started telling my closest friends and family, and it spread to everyone pretty quick.

Most of my friends and family were awesome about it. But I started noticing a lot of changes from my teammates. It wasn't much — it was small stuff, like the day I realized nobody was putting their stuff next to mine anymore in the change room. A few weeks later, nobody was coming within a ten-foot-radius of me in the change room, as if I had some invisible plague and they didn't want to get too close to it.

And when we were playing, things were different, too. Everyone used to high-five or hug after a good rally on the court, and if we won we'd all start hugging each other. But after I came out, it was like everyone was trying to keep me at arm's length. If I went for a hug they'd hold their hand out for a high-five. If I went for a high-five, sometimes they'd pretend not to see it and turn away.

Nobody ever mentioned it, and no way was I going to bring it up. That would look so bad on my part — *gay girl complains that her female teammates aren't hugging her enough!*

I did talk about it with one of my best friends, Alexis, who's also on the team. But every time I mentioned it to her, she would brush it off and say she never noticed anything.

"I don't know what you're talking about," Alexis said. "You're exaggerating. Nobody is *avoiding* touching you."

All those subtle little things — my teammates avoiding me, nobody hugging me anymore, girls jumping out of the way in the change room — are microaggressions. It wasn't much — it was small stuff, but it hurt me.

And then there was my nickname. Our whole team has always had nicknames for each other — mine used to be Wilson, which is my last name and also a volleyball brand. After I came out, they stopped calling me Wilson and started calling me Gaykenzie instead. They said it was a "loving nickname."

"We're allowed to joke like this because we're allies!" Olivia, one of my teammates, would say.

Everyone would always laugh. I would laugh too, because if I wasn't laughing with them, it would have just felt like I was getting laughed at.

It still kinda felt like I was getting laughed at, though.

At the end of the season, our team captain, Meaghan, hosted a sleepover for the whole team to celebrate our second-place finish in the standings. I guess she and the co-captains discussed it and decided not to invite me.

The part that hurt most was that none of my teammates had mentioned it to me — not even Alexis. I learned about it later that night watching their Insta stories and a team TikTok.

I talked to Meaghan the next Monday in school, and she told me that she thought I wouldn't have wanted to come because she "didn't have enough space for me to have my own room. And obviously you wouldn't want to share with anyone, right?"

I had no idea what that even *meant*, but I walked away almost in tears. After that, I decided, I was done. If they were going to act like this, I didn't want to be on the team again next year. You still have to try out, at the start of each year, but if you were on the team in grade nine, it's almost guaranteed they take you back for grade ten. And I'm a good player. I'd be a shoo-in.

But I don't care. I've had enough.

* * *

When the buzzer goes for the final time, I find myself looking up with disappointment. We have a group hug, which I join in, my shoulders tense, and then we line up to shake hands with the other team.

It's a regional volleyball camp and we all come from different high schools in the area. We've been playing together for the last three weeks, but none of the people here know I'm gay. I didn't want to tell them, just in case they were weird about it.

But I've gotten increasingly paranoid that not telling anyone means that *I'm* being weird about it. Now, when people go for high-fives or reach to help me up, I'll accept their hand but duck away as fast as possible. Some of the girls have hung out a few times over the summer, and I was always invited. But every time, I found myself saying I was busy.

I don't know why, really. It just felt easier.

After getting changed, I walk to the gym's exit doors. Another girl, Sydney, happens to be leaving at the same time, and we walk together.

"Are you coming out tonight?" Sydney asks.

A bunch of the girls are hanging out, as a sort of celebration or goodbye or whatever. The plan for the evening is in our group chat. I think it's gourmet waffles and a movie at the drive-in.

"No," I say, shaking my head. "I, um, have to help my sister with something."

"Ah, too bad," Sydney says, just as we reach the gym doors. "Well . . . have a good year."

"Thanks," I say.

She waves and walks off, getting into a car with who must have been her mum and two younger sisters.

I start scanning the parking lot. My own sister told me she'd pick me up today. A moment later Grace pulls up and I climb into the passenger seat.

"How was it?" she asks.

"You know . . ." I say, shrugging. "It was fine."

CHAPTER TWO

Inclusive Leagues

"Kids! Come help me set up for dinner!"

I find it funny when my mom calls us "kids" — my oldest brother, Noah, is going into his third year of uni; Grace is starting grade twelve; I'm starting grade ten; and my little brother, Tommy, will be starting grade nine.

I find my mom in the kitchen, and Tommy appears a second behind me. "Beat ya," I mutter to him, and he flicks me in the head. As Grace and Noah filter in, more slowly, Mom puts us all to work: Noah husking corn, Grace chopping veggies for a tray, and Tommy and I are tasked with setting everything on the table — salads, drinks, cutlery, condiments — for people to grab and take their plates outside. My parents have invited my aunt, uncle, and cousins over for a barbecue tonight, to celebrate our final day of summer before school starts again.

My dad walks into the kitchen and yells "Think fast!" before throwing a basketball at Noah. Noah catches it but drops the corn, and sends the bowl of husks clattering to the floor.

"Nice," Dad says.

"Uh, I'm holding a *knife* here!" Grace yells.

"Steve, can you take it outside, please?" Mom asks.

"All right," Dad says, with a sigh. He holds up his hands and Noah passes the ball back to him. "But don't blame me when I crush you in our family basketball game later."

"Noah — stop throwing that!" Grace says.

"Steve, outside, please," Mom says again.

Dad shrugs and takes it outside.

Mom sighs. "I'm going to check on the barbecue," she says, and walks outside. A moment later we can hear the sound of dribbling through the open window.

Tommy, midway through pulling cutlery from a drawer, walks over and peers out the window. "They're playing," he says, sounding shocked. He leans closer and yells through the screen, "Hey! We're making dinner in here!"

"Be there in a minute!" Mom calls back.

Meet my family: tall, sporty, annoying.

"Well," Tommy says, walking back to the table and dumping forks on it. "If anyone asks why we're so competitive, that's where we get it from."

"Competitive and insane," I mutter.

"Oh, shut it," Grace says. "You're the most competitive of all of us."

"I am not!"

"Yeah, right. How many service aces did you have last year?"

"Twenty-one," I reply automatically, because she's right — I am competitive and obviously I know all my own stats. I could tell you all my stats from the year before, too, and the year before that. It's not even that I want to be the best or beat records or something — I'm just always trying to be better than my last year of playing.

"Exactly," Grace says, pointing the knife at me. "Competitive. There's no way you're not playing this year."

"Don't point the knife at me," I snap. "And I'm not."

I've been telling my family all summer that I'm not trying out for volleyball again this fall, but Grace keeps refusing to believe me.

"Come on, Kenz," she says. "*Come on*. You're seriously not going to play this year?"

"I'm not going to play," I tell her firmly. "No cap. I'm done with volleyball."

"I know I've said it already, but you should play, Kenzie," Noah says. "You're too good. And you want to keep it up — you could try to play in uni, or even intramurals. It's a great way to meet people."

"Seriously, you're going to regret not playing," Grace says.

"Thanks for all telling me how to live my life," I say, irritated. "Tommy? You want to chime in here, too?"

He shrugs. "I think you're right, Kenzie."

I'm stunned. "You do?"

"Yeah. Those girls treated you like crap. Why would you want to play with them?"

I feel a smile curling at the corner of my mouth. "Thanks, Tom."

"But I think you're going to miss playing," he adds.

"Ugh."

They're being stupid. It's not like I was some Olympic-level player. Am I good? Yes. Do I love the game? Yes. But it's not the only thing in my life. Maybe I want more time to do other stuff, or meet new people . . . maybe even go on a date or something . . .

I'm saved from further conversation about my dead volleyball career by the sound of the doorbell. A moment later, the door opens and feet come clattering in, several voices all calling out to us at once.

"Hello, anyone home?"

"Wilsons!"

"We're here!"

Our cousins have arrived. Thank god.

* * *

Luckily once my cousins are here, everyone moves on from talking about how I'm not going for volleyball — they have more interesting stuff to talk about. My aunt Sarah has stories to share from her latest work drama (one of her co-workers is getting catfished, but refuses to believe it). My cousin Josie is about to start her first year of college and moves to St. Catharines tomorrow. My uncle Phil ran his lawnmower into a rock not once, but three different times in August, and has decided to start paying the kid next door to do their lawn.

But the most interesting thing comes up during dinner. We're sitting in lawn chairs in the backyard, balancing plates with burgers, corn, and potato salad on our laps, most of us broken up into smaller conversations.

I'm talking to my cousin Mia about her on-again off-again boyfriend, Bryce. (Josie, on the other side of Mia, is actively trying not to roll her eyes behind her.) Mia's twenty and has been dating him since she was fifteen.

I'm pretty wrapped up in the tea, and I'm mostly ignoring the snippets of conversation I hear floating over from other people's conversations: *"inclusive . . ." "this year . . ." "work's good . . ."*

Suddenly I hear my name and turn slightly to see Noah waving at me. "Hey, Kenzie, you listening to this?" he says. "It's really cool."

Noah gestures to my cousin Jamie, who's sitting next to him. Jamie is our oldest cousin — he's twenty-six and lives in Hamilton. He's also the only cousin in my family — other than me — who's gay.

"I was just telling your brother about the inclusive softball league I played in this summer," Jamie says.

"What's that?" I ask.

"It's a league that's all about the queer community," Jamie explains, and now almost all of the other conversations have fallen quiet, listening to him. "Allies are welcome to join, too, but the idea is that it's a safe place for 2SLGBTQIA+ people to play."

"Huh," I say, my mind spinning. "I didn't know that type of stuff even existed."

"It's pretty new, but it's really fun!" Jamie says. "We had all sorts of special events, where you'd dress up for the game, sometimes people would show up in drag . . ."

"I don't get it," my aunt Sarah interrupts. "I mean, I'm glad you had fun, but why do LGBT-Q-2-Q—" she stumbles over the acronym "—why do these people need their own league, anyway? Shouldn't we just try to make *every* softball or sports league as welcoming as possible? Shouldn't they all be safe to play in?"

What she's just said makes my blood boil, because, *duh.* Yes, obviously that would be nice. But obviously it's not happening, either, or I'd still be on the volleyball team. And I know that what I've had to deal with isn't even that bad compared to some stuff. Jamie's told me stories from when he was in high school — people saying things like "go, fag, go!" when he was running, people stealing his clothes when he was in gym so that he'd have to wear his sweaty gym clothes the rest of the day, people writing "fruity" and "tranny boy" on his running shoes.

And Jamie is Sarah's son! How does she not know this? How does she not get it? I have to set down my plate and shove my hands under my legs to hide their shaking.

When Jamie replies, though, his voice is steady. "Ideally, yeah, every space would be safe," he says. "But it's not, yet. And sometimes it's just reassuring, you know, to be in a league and know that everybody who's there is committed to making it a welcoming, safe space."

Sarah makes a noise like, "Hmm." Jamie just ignores her and keeps talking.

"It's nice to be able to play and not worry that one jerk in the crowd is going to yell something that ruins your day," he says. "And it's not just for queer people, you know. Allies can join. It's about building community. I met a lot of new friends this summer through it."

"That's sick," Noah says. "I'd like to join, if it runs next year. I'll be at McMaster all summer doing my co-op."

"Yeah? It should," Jamie says. "I'll send you the link . . ."

The conversation moves on. After dinner we have cake. My mom lights candles on it and lets Tommy blow out the candles for no other reason than "he's starting high school!" We play a game of Wilson vs. Gaudon family basketball, and my insanely competitive family wins by a mile. I play okay — basketball's not my sport — but I miss a couple of easy shots. My mind is elsewhere.

At the end of the night, as we're hugging them goodbye in the driveway, I go to hug Jamie. Before he climbs into their car, I gently touch his arm and ask quietly, "Hey, what was the name of that league you joined this summer?"

He leans over and says, quietly smiling, "It was the Steel City Inclusive Softball Association. Look it up, baby gay."

"Thanks," I say, smiling. He gives me a second hug and then climbs into the car. My family stands in the driveway, waving them goodbye as they drive away.

CHAPTER THREE
Searching

Later that night, I look up the Steel City Inclusive Softball Association. And then I spend the rest of the night falling into a rabbit hole of looking at other leagues online.

I had no idea there were so many.

There's the one in Hamilton, and there's also the softball-playing Mabel League in Vancouver, the Cabbagetown Group Softball League in Toronto, and the Calgary Apollo Softball Association.

There's the Edmonton Rage LGBT+ Hockey league in Alberta, the Toronto Gay Hockey Association, Queer Hockey Nova Scotia, and The Cutting Edges LGBTQ+ Hockey Association in Vancouver.

There are fifteen different curling leagues across Canada,

from the Pacific Rim Curling in Vancouver to Prairie Lily Curling in Saskatoon to the Loose Ends in Halifax. There's even an annual Canadian Pride Curling Championship tournament, where all fifteen teams can compete to be national champions.

There's the Front Runners, an international group of LGBTQ+ running and walking clubs, with chapter clubs in Calgary, Vancouver, Winnipeg, St. John's, Halifax, London, Ottawa, Toronto, Quebec City, and Montreal.

I can't believe how much is out there — and that I had *no idea* any of this existed. Jamie's right — I am a baby gay.

On one of the pages, I find stats from an international study of nearly 9,500 gay and straight people. It was reviewed by seven international academics and says it was the largest of its kind. It says they talked to more than twelve thousand lesbian, gay, bisexual, and transgender participants, from Canada, the States, Australia, New Zealand, and all the EU countries.

The stats say that eighty percent of participants have witnessed or experienced homophobia in sport, with homophobic language the most common (yep, me too).

Eighty-four percent of gay men and eighty-two percent of lesbians have heard verbal slurs such as "faggot" or "dyke" (yep, also me).

Eighty percent believe gay people are "not at all accepted"

or "accepted a little" or only "moderately accepted" in sporting culture (I mean, I quit the volleyball team. So yeah, duh).

I wish I could send this link to Aunt Sarah. It's like the perfect response to what she said earlier — why do we need these leagues? This is why!

Maybe I should send her the link . . .

I smile at the thought, but decide not to stir up family drama — for now. Instead, I search to see if there are any queer sport leagues near me.

There's a league nearby, run by the Forest City Sport and Social Club in London, but you have to be at least nineteen years old to join.

I try changing my search: *queer sports league ontario for teens.*

No results.

I try a few times with different keywords. *LGBTQ2S+ sport league, queer volleyball league, queer sports league near me.*

Nada. I guess I should have expected that. Almost all the leagues I found are for adults, not teens. And most of them are in big cities, not small towns like Ilderton. I'm surprised that London even has one.

My eyes are burning from staring at the screen for so long. Finally, exhausted, I turn off my phone and set it on my nightstand. Feeling the weirdest mix of excited and dejected, I go to sleep.

CHAPTER FOUR

Brooklyn

"Mackenzie!"

It's the first day of school, lunch period. I've just walked into the doors of the cafeteria when I hear a familiar voice calling my name.

"*Mackenzie*!" I turn just in time and then my other best friend, Skye, barrels into me in a massive hug. I hug her back.

"Oh my god," she says, releasing me. "I feel like I haven't seen you all summer. How was volleyball camp?"

"Eh," I shrug. "It was good. Same as last year, really."

"Have you seen Alexis?"

"Yeah, we had homeroom together," I say. "Have you seen her?"

"Not yet!" Skye says. We both start craning our necks,

looking for her. A few moments later we've found her and are sitting at our favourite table by the windows.

We catch up on all the latest news: I haven't seen either of them since before volleyball camp started, and Alexis has been gone most of the summer at her family's cottage. We've been messaging daily, but it's not the same as seeing each other for real.

Alexis tells us about her last couple weeks at the cottage, which mostly revolved around sneaking out to parties across the lake. Skye tells us about the last few weeks of her summer job. She was working for a coffee truck and spent every weekend working at a different festival with them. I tell them about volleyball camp, skipping over the parts where I avoided making any friends. Eventually, I get to telling them about the barbecue with my cousins last weekend.

"My cousin Jamie was telling me about this softball league he joined over the summer," I say.

"Jamie's the gay one, right?" Alexis asks.

"Yeah."

"I love him," Alexis says. "He's so fun."

"He is," I say. "Anyway, it wasn't just a normal league — it was an inclusive league. So it was for queer people and all about creating a safe space to play. Apparently it was really fun."

"That sounds sick," Skye says. "So wait — could anyone join, or just queer people?"

"This one, it was anyone, but everyone had to be, like, committed to making it a safe space. But allies were welcome," I say.

"*This* one?"

"Yeah — I looked it up and apparently there are a ton of leagues like this all over the country. I got really into looking it up last night," I admit. "Some are like the one Jamie joined — they take queer people and allies — and some are just for queer people. They exist for so many different sports, too. Like there's softball, and I also found a bunch of leagues for hockey, a weird amount for curling, a ton of running clubs . . ."

"Any for volleyball?" Skye asks, smiling.

"No," I say. "I wish."

"What do you mean, you wish?" Alexis says. "You're already going to be playing on the junior girls' volleyball team at school — would you even have time for another league?"

Oh, shit. I totally forgot to tell Alexis.

"Um," I say, dropping my eyes to my lunch. "I'm not, uh — I'm not going to go out for the team this year."

"*What*?" Alexis is so loud that people at the table next to ours look up.

I glance up and meet her eyes, guiltily. "Sorry, I should

have told you earlier. I just — I, um, don't want to do it this year."

"So what? You're just done with it? You're just done with the whole team?"

"It's not that big of a deal," I say.

"Of course it is! You've literally *abandoned* me!"

"I haven't abandoned you, Jesus Christ! I just want to try something different this year."

"Like what, gay volleyball?"

"There is no gay volleyball," I say, frustrated.

"Only when you play it," Alexis snaps, and I feel my cheeks flame. We both fall silent, and Skye glances anxiously between us.

Eventually, Skye says, hesitantly, "It's okay if Mackenzie doesn't want to play anymore . . . I mean, the team was kind of, um, you know, a bit awful to her last year . . ."

"You aren't even on the team — how would you know?" Alexis snaps. She stands up and grabs her bag. "I have to get to my next class."

"Come on, Alexis— " I say.

"No. It's fine. You don't have to play, alright? Have fun sitting on the sidelines this year."

"Alexis!" Skye says.

Alexis ignores us and walks away. Skye and I are left alone, and a minute later she reaches out and squeezes my hand.

"She took that well," Skye says, and I laugh.

"I should have told her earlier," I say. "I feel awful."

"Maybe," Skye says. "But you know she'll get over it. I'm sure she's just disappointed that you guys won't get to play together this year."

"Yeah," I say. "Honestly . . . don't tell anyone, but I'm going to really miss playing this year, myself."

"Seriously? I thought you, like, *hated* being on the team last year."

"I didn't *hate* it — I mean — it was just little stuff that sort of built up — and yeah, I'm not going to miss *that* experience. I don't want to have to relive it this year. I'm glad I'm not playing. But . . . you know . . . I still love the game. I wish I could play, somehow, just like . . . with a good group."

It's something I can't say to anyone else because I know if I admitted that I don't want to stop playing, anyone else would try to convince me to just play, already, with the school team. If I said this stuff to my family, or Alexis, they'd tell me I was being too dramatic, or making way too much of everything that happened last year.

But Skye is the best. She just listens and nods.

"That sucks," she says. "What about those inclusive leagues, though?"

"What about them?"

"Maybe you should join one. If you miss playing."

"I told you, there's no volleyball one. *And* they're all for adults. None for people our age."

"Well," Skye says, "maybe you should start one, then."

* * *

I'm planning on apologizing to Alexis in fourth period. We shared our class schedules with each other in our group chat with Skye, and we signed up for certain classes to be together, so I know we'll both be in fourth-period German. But when I get there, she's already sitting at a table of two with Meaghan, our volleyball captain from last year.

I pause for a minute, unsure what to do. Alexis briefly catches my eye, pointedly shifts so that she's not looking at me anymore, and goes back to talking to Meaghan.

Okay. She's still mad, then.

Trying to not let it bother me, I sit down at an empty table on the other side of the classroom. Fine — if she doesn't want to talk, we don't have to talk.

With three minutes to go until the bell, people start filing in. Nobody sits next to me and I'm starting to worry that I'll have to sit here alone, looking like a total loser. I bring out my phone and message Skye quickly. *alexis won't sit with me.*

I'm watching my phone for a reply. One minute until the bell.

"Okay to share?"

I glance up, feeling a whoosh of relief, and then my stomach drops.

It's Brooklyn.

Like stunningly gorgeous, girl on the basketball team, my biggest crush, Brooklyn.

I can't make myself say anything, so I just nod, mutely. She gives me kind of an odd smile and sits down.

She's a year older than me, but the German class in our school is small — the class ends up being a grade ten and eleven split class most years. I guess this is one of those years.

Angling my screen so that she can't see, I quickly send Skye another message: *BROOKLYN IS SITTING NEXT TO ME.*

The bell goes and I quickly tuck my phone into my backpack on the floor.

She's right next to me. She smells so good. Oh my god.

Ms. Martin, at the front of the room, starts talking and everyone sort of settles down. The first day you're always on a sort of high from seeing everyone again and being back in school. As we got to the end of the day, I felt like things were starting to chill . . . but with Brooklyn sitting next to me, suddenly I feel more alert than I have all day.

I'm trying so hard to be normal. I'm focused on looking at the front of the room as Ms. Martin speaks, introducing us all to the class and what we're going to learn over the next semester. Nodding along. Picking up the German textbook she's left at each seat and pretending to flip through it.

In between, I sneak glimpses of Brooklyn out of the corner of my eye. She's literally stunning: athletic, tall, and graceful. She has long blond hair, but it's dirty blond, not pale blond like mine. Today she's wearing jeans, grey Converse, and a black crop top with yellow words scrawled on it: *girls gone mild.*

I've known her since last year. I went to Oxbow Elementary in Ilderton from kindergarten to grade eight — that's where I met Alexis and Skye. But Ilderton is too small to have its own high school, so we all started bussing to Medway High School in Arva, just north of London, in grade nine.

I still remember seeing her for the first time at orientation last August. Everyone had nervous jitters from being in a new school, with a ton of new people. But she seemed so calm, so relaxed, walking around in shorts and a loose white T-shirt, chatting easily with people. I've been crushing on her pretty much non-stop since.

Our high school is way bigger than Oxbow, but it's still small enough that you can know — or know of — everyone in your grade. You eventually have a class with everyone, or see them around, or have a mutual friend.

Or, in my case, watch from afar and notice everything.

Here's everything I know about Brooklyn: she plays starting forward on the basketball team. She has a group of friends that she's nearly always with; I don't know any of their names, but I recognize them all by now. She seems funny; like a life-of-the-party person. She moves her hands a lot when she talks. Sometimes she takes the bus. I think she got her license last spring, because in May, she's occasionally driven to school in a small green car. After school, she's sometimes wearing a backwards baseball cap, but she doesn't wear it at school (we have a "no hats in class" rule). She's from a small town, too — I think Thorndale. She sprained her ankle last winter and used crutches for a couple weeks.

She's also gay. Did I mention she's gay? In case the basketball team, Converse sneakers, and backwards hats weren't enough clues for you.

I rate her so high, but we have different friend groups, and I've always been too shy to just walk up and talk to her. And now, sitting next to her, I feel tongue-tied.

Towards the end of class, Ms. Martin gives us five minutes of "discussion time."

"Staying at your tables, I want you to practice introducing yourself and talking about your day," Ms. Martin says. "And if you're at different levels, that's okay! You can help each other."

The class erupts into conversation while Ms. Martin sits down at her desk and looks at her computer.

I glance over at Brooklyn, who's looking back at me. "So, uh . . ." I ask, "Um . . . how are you?"

Brooklyn looks at me, a smile playing on her lips. "Um . . . in German?"

"Oops," I say, and I blush. "Uh, uh . . . *wie geht's*?"

"I'm just messing with you," Brooklyn says, laughing, and relieved, I laugh too. "Honestly, I forgot everything we learned last year over the summer."

"You didn't spend your whole summer practicing German?" I deadpan, and she laughs.

"Nope. I mostly hung out with friends, played a lot of basketball in my driveway. Saw a lot of movies. What about you? What did you do this summer?"

I can't believe I'm having a conversation with her. Like a totally normal, ordinary conversation.

"I went to volleyball camp," I say. "And . . . watched a lot of TV. Hung out with my siblings. That's about it."

"Oh, yeah. You're like, into volleyball, right?"

"Um, sort of," I say.

I don't add anything more — I don't really want to get into it.

"Cool," she says, after a beat.

The bell rings, and we both look up. At the front of the room, Ms. Martin stands and reminds us to all take our textbooks home and go through the first chapter and practice questions tonight.

Brooklyn stands up, swinging her bag over her shoulder and grabbing her book.

"See you later," she says.

"Oh, yeah, uh — see you," I say. I watch her go for a minute and then quickly stop watching. I don't want anyone to see me staring after her. I pick up the textbook and flip through the pages, then slowly stuff it in my backpack and stand up.

I remember, too late, that I should try and talk to Alexis. I feel like I should apologize to her before the end of the day. I feel bad that I didn't tell her earlier that I wasn't doing volleyball this year. But when I turn to look at where she was sitting, she's already gone.

Sighing, I exit the classroom, making my way through the hallways and heading to catch the bus alone.

CHAPTER FIVE

Trying Out

A few weeks later, I'm at the doors of the cafeteria, waiting for Skye. The lunch period's just started for junior students (grade nine and ten) and there's a ton of people moving into the caf, so I'm standing to the side, out of the rush.

I spot Alexis in the crowd and smile at her, giving her a little wave. She smiles back and comes over. We're good now — she was upset about the volleyball thing for, like, a week.

We made up since then, and it's all back to normal . . . except for fourth-period German class, where I still sit with Brooklyn. But that's not my fault. The first week, Alexis kept snubbing me to sit with Meaghan. Honestly, I didn't care, because every time the seat beside me stayed empty, Brooklyn would come and sit next to me.

Then Alexis and I made up, and I figured we'd sit together again. But the first day after we made up, Brooklyn beat Alexis to class and took the seat next to me. And she's taken it every day since, too.

Now, Alexis walks over and says hi. "Should we go get our table?"

"Oh, I'm waiting for Skye. We're actually going to talk to Ms. Arsenault about the league. Do you want to come?"

After a few weeks of deliberation and talking endlessly about it with Skye, Alexis, and my sister, I've decided to try and make an inclusive league happen. Alexis said she was probably too busy with volleyball to get involved, but Skye's on board with me. We've filled out the "new club" form, but before we can hand it into the office, we need to get a staff sponsor to sign it. We're going to try asking Ms. Arsenault today.

Alexis shakes her head. "No, that's your thing. I see Cassie and Emma in there — I'll go sit with them."

"Okay. We'll find you later?"

"Yeah, let me know when you're done with Ms. Arsenault and we'll meet up."

She joins the rush of people into the cafeteria. I only have to wait another minute before Skye turns up, a little breathless.

"Hey! Ready?" she asks.

"Ready," I say. Suddenly I feel weirdly nervous and excited.

"I can't believe we're doing this," Skye says as we start walking down the hall.

"Same," I say. "I'm, like, shaking."

"God, I hope she says yes."

"Me too. I'm sure she will. You have the form, right?"

"Yeah. Right here," Skye says, pulling it out of her bag and handing it to me.

We picked Ms. Arsenault *very* intentionally — we talked about it for ages and both agreed that she's the teacher who is most likely to be enthusiastic about volunteering her time for this with us. We had her last year for French, and she was super cool. But it's not just that. It's also the fact that she hangs a giant pride flag in her classroom, and refuses to take it down.

Our school is clearly trying to be part of this decade, and talks about values and diversity and equality so much it's irritating. We have speakers every September who talk about discrimination and safe spaces and being accepting. We even have a cringe-worthy gay alliance club, although I think they're called the "Belonging Club."

But we also have a lot of rural families who come here. Small towns can be a bit old school sometimes — I know, I live in one. And there's pockets of liberal people, and people who really support good stuff, and I'm sure it's better than it was, like, twenty years ago. But there's also still the odd person who's super religious, or doesn't really believe in marriage equality, or gets really furious when a trans girl plays on a girl's sports team.

One of those people caused problems for Ms. Arsenault last year. The whole school knew about it. Their kid was in Ms. Arsenault's homeroom, and when they went for a parent-teacher meeting they saw the pride flag that hangs at the back of her classroom. They asked her to take it down and she said no. The next day, the parent went to the principal and asked for the flag to be taken down, and our principal backed up Ms. Arsenault and also said no. I think the parent went all the way to the school board, and they got a whole group of people complaining about it. There was an online petition that was called something idiotic, like "Neutrality in our Schools for Nonbiased Teachers!"

People talked about it for a long time, even though I don't think anything really happened in the end. The student eventually transferred to a different school. Ms. Arsenault's flag stayed up.

I don't even know if she's gay, or just a *really* committed ally. But either way, I think if there's a teacher who would be excited about our club, it would be her.

We're hoping that she'll still be in her classroom at the start of lunch. When we get to her door, Skye and I both take a deep breath. We glance at each other one last time, as if we're checking — *you really want to do this?*

I nod a little, and then Skye reaches out and knocks on the door. It's partly ajar and swings the rest of the way open with Skye's knock.

"Come in," Ms. Arsenault calls.

We step inside and walk up to her desk. She's sitting at her computer, eating her lunch.

"Mackenzie, Skye! *Bonjour, c'est un plaisir de vous revoir*! *Ça va*?" she says.

Oh, crap. I didn't sign up for French this year. And I *definitely* don't remember anything from last year.

Ms. Arsenault laughs at our expressions. "It's okay — you don't need to speak *en français*. You're not in my class anymore, so I won't put you to the test. How can I help you two?"

I take a deep breath, and then briefly explain: we're starting a volleyball league for 2SLGBTQIA+ teens. It's so that queer teens can have a safe space to play. Allies can join too, as long as they promise to help make it inclusive.

"Skye and I have filled out the form as co-chairs," I say. "We just need a staff sponsor to sign off and agree to supervise our meetings — or games, I guess — basically."

Her face hasn't changed much at all as I've been talking. Now, I hold out the form to her.

She takes it, and spends what feels like a very long time reading it.

Finally, she clears her throat.

"How often do you plan to meet? I mean, play?"

Skye and I glance at each other. "Uh, I think once a week?"

"After school?"

"Yeah, I think so."

"What day?"

"We're thinking Tuesdays? Or Thursdays? But, like, whenever."

She nods, picks up a pen, and signs it quickly, then hands it back.

That was fast.

Holding my breath, I reach out and take the signed form. I almost can't believe it. I glance over at Skye, who raises her eyebrows at me, then back at Ms. Arsenault.

"Thank you — thanks, we really — thank you."

"Of course," Ms. Arsenault says, and she smiles again. "This is a great idea, you two. Well done for taking the initiative. If you need anything, let me know."

I nod, tell her thanks again, and then Skye and I walk out of the classroom.

We wait until we're halfway down the hall before we look at each other.

"That took, like, two minutes," Skye says, glancing at the time on her phone.

"I know!" I say. "I can't believe it was that easy."

"Let's hope everything else is, too," Skye says, grinning at me.

We go straight to the main office and drop off the form at the front desk with the secretary. Then we go for lunch, talking excitedly. I almost can't believe it — we're going to start the league. It's really going to happen!

CHAPTER SIX

Benched

About a week later, my homeroom teacher, Mr. Moore, hands me an envelope with my name on it, and tells me it came from the office for me. He seems just as confused as I am.

When I open it, I realize that it's our new club application form. My heart jumps. There's something new added to it. At the bottom, in red pen, someone has written: *Please come to Mr. Stapleton's office when available.*

What the heck?

"It says I'm supposed to go to the vice principal's office," I tell Mr. Moore.

"Okay," he says, still looking confused. "Off you go, then."

I leave class and start walking to the main office. Partway there, I hesitate, thinking. I double back and go upstairs, to

Ms. Arsenault's classroom.

There's no class in there, but she's sitting at her desk and looks up when I knock lightly on the door. I show her the form.

"I just got it," I say, "I don't know what's up, but I'm going to the office now."

"Okay," she says, nodding, and stands up. "This is my planning period. I can come with you, if you like?"

"Yeah. Please."

At the main office, we tell the secretary we're here to see Mr. Stapleton. She has us take a seat on the bench outside his office. Skye is already waiting there for us and just gives me a baffled shrug when I ask if she knows what's going on. We only have to wait a few minutes before he appears at the door, gesturing for us to come in.

"What can I help you three with?" he asks. We all sit down, him behind the desk and us on the other side.

"I got this?" I say, passing him the form. "It just said to come see you."

"It's for the new inclusive volleyball club," Ms. Arsenault says.

"*Ah*," he says. He takes the form from me and quickly scans it before setting it down. "Who's Mackenzie, and who's Skye?"

"I'm Mackenzie."

"Okay. Nice to meet you both. Well, first off, I have to say, what a fantastic idea for the club! I applaud you for bringing this to our school. I have one concern, though, which is that people may give you some complaints about the *name* of the club."

After much deliberation, we submitted the club name as "Gays and Slays Volleyball League."

"I think we can get rid of this concern, though, by simply changing the name of the club," Mr. Stapleton continues.

"Uh, changing it to what?" I ask.

"Oh, that's up to you," he says. "You know, something simple like the 'Inclusive Volleyball Club,' or the 'Fun for Everyone Volleyball League.'"

"What's wrong with the club name they chose?" Ms. Arsenault asks.

He hesitates. "Well . . . you know, we've had a few complaints in the last year about different DEI initiatives we're doing. And obviously the school is fully supportive of a club that makes space for everyone to enjoy sport. I'm just concerned that, if the club goes ahead with this name, it's going to trigger some negative responses, and that blowback will be aimed at you two— " he gestures to me and Skye " —which isn't fair. But again, you can totally start the club, just with a slightly changed name. Like, again, the 'Fun for Everyone Volleyball League' or 'Volleyball For All.'"

He smiles at us. He seems to think these are very good suggestions.

But I don't know what to say. Calling it the "Inclusive Volleyball Club" would still get the point across. But somehow it feels wrong. We put a lot of thought into the club name. We wanted it to showcase that it's fun, and chill, and for us — not a random school thing that's just being done to check a box.

The thought of changing the name makes me feel so upset, but I'm worried I'm overreacting. I don't want to fight this for no reason. Beside me, Skye is sitting quietly, not speaking. I have no idea what she's thinking.

"Um . . . I'm not sure," I say.

"Okay," he says. "That's alright. Do you want to maybe think about it for a bit, and then you can resubmit the form?"

Skye glances over at me, and I shrug. "Um . . . okay."

Smiling, he leans across the desk. I take the form back from him, and it feels like a failure.

Going to leave, I pause at the door. Skye is right behind me, but Ms. Arsenault hasn't moved from her chair.

She catches my eye and waves. "Go ahead, you two. I'll meet you in the hall in a minute. I just have to talk to Mr. Stapleton quick about something."

Skye and I head out. I go to close the door and at the last second, leave it open half an inch, hoping they won't notice, as

Skye and I take a seat on the bench outside his office.

A moment later, I hear them start to speak again. Their voices are still perfectly clear; I smile.

"Okay," Ms. Arsenault says. "What exactly is the issue with the club name?"

"Come on, Katie," Mr. Stapleton says. "'Gays and Slays'? You understand the scrutiny that these types of things can come under. Even if we just call it an inclusive league, you *know* that some parents are going to complain. We had all those complaints last year about the pride flag you hung up."

"It was three complaints, which is not actually a huge amount considering our student body is over a thousand," Ms. Arsenault says. "If anything, I think it shows that more parents are in support of the pride flag than against it."

"And of course they are," Mr. Stapleton says. "I am, too. You know I am. But I'm just trying to avoid causing any problems with this as much as possible. And I'm trying to avoid causing any problems for you or Mackenzie and Skye. I like the idea. I think it's a great idea for a club. You just need to change the name to something a little more neutral, and I'll approve it."

"That's it? Those are the only options you're providing? Change the name or we don't get approved?"

"I'm saying change the name, and I'll approve it. Now, is there anything else I can help you with?"

"I guess not," Ms. Arsenault says. "Have a good afternoon."

"You, too," he says. "Thanks, Katie. I appreciate you working with me on this."

The door opens, and Ms. Arsenault comes out. She closes it firmly behind her, shutting it properly this time. She meets my eye and Skye and I both stand up. We walk out of the office together and partway down the hall, until we reach a bench, far out of earshot of the office now. She gestures at the bench and we both sit down.

"You heard all that?" Ms. Arsenault asks us, and we nod.

"Yeah," I say. "Thanks for, you know, asking him about it."

"Sure," she says. "So . . . what are you two thinking?"

"I dunno," I say, staring at my shoes. "I guess . . . I don't know, maybe we were being naive, I just thought they'd approve it. I didn't think the name would be an issue."

"Neither did I," Skye says.

"It shouldn't have been," Ms. Arsenault says. "Not today. I'm sorry."

"So . . . what now? Do we change the club name?"

"Well," Ms. Arsenault says, "do you want to change the club name?"

"I don't know," I say. "It feels weird to, like, die on this hill or whatever . . . it's just the name. But it feels like it changes the whole mood of the club or something, you know?"

“Yeah,” Skye says. “And do we even want to run a club called ‘Volleyball For All?’”

Ms. Arsenault laughs, and we laugh too.

“Fair enough,” she says. “You can think about it. When you’re ready, let me know whatever you decide to do. And if you want to keep trying to get the club approved under the original name, just know you have my support. If we press it, he may just back down.”

“Thanks, Ms. Arsenault.”

“No problem,” she says. She stands up to go. “You two can take a minute, if you like, and then head back to class, okay?”

“Okay.”

Skye reaches over and squeezes my hand. “I should probably get back to class,” she says. “I’m supposed to be running lines with someone right now. You okay?”

“Yeah, yeah. Go,” I say.

She heads down the hall, too, and I’m left sitting alone on the bench. The hall is quiet, aside from the occasional footfall. Everyone’s in class right now.

I’m trying not to feel super upset, but it’s hard. I had so many ideas about the league. Skye and I had already started planning how we were going to organize it — we’d even brainstormed some ideas for special events, like dressing up for a game on Halloween. I guess we really got ahead of ourselves.

"Mackenzie?"

I look up at the sound of my name, and to my shock, it's Brooklyn.

She's standing a few feet away from my bench, wearing track pants and a t-shirt, backpack over one shoulder. I was so wrapped up in my thoughts that I must not have heard her walk up.

"Hey," I say.

"Are you okay?" she asks.

"I'm okay, I guess," I say. "Just . . . life, you know."

She comes over and sits down next to me, setting her bag on the ground. "You look . . . a little upset."

"Yeah. I am. It's just . . ." I hesitate. For a moment, I'm not sure what to say, or how to explain it.

Then I meet her eyes. She's so beautiful. She raises her eyebrows a little as if she's asking a question. But she's just waiting, patiently, listening.

In a rush, I find myself telling her all about the league. How Skye and I filled out the form and got Ms. Arsenault to be a staff sponsor, and how I thought that meant we were going to be starting a club. But now Mr. Stapleton's said we have to change the name, and I'm not sure what to do next, or if I'm overthinking it all.

"I don't know if I want to still run it and call it something boring — because also, like, where's the line? Are we able to say certain things when we tell people about the club, or do we have to take anything fun off, like, a poster? And if it's supposed to be a fun space to play volleyball and make people feel welcomed, doesn't changing the name defeat the whole *point* of having an inclusive league?"

I finish and take a deep breath. "Oh my god. I'm sorry. That was a lot."

"No! God, don't be . . . don't be sorry. That really sucks, the VP saying you have to change the name. And I get it. You know, why you don't want to change the name."

"Thanks," I say. "That means a lot."

"Of course. And do you want to know what I think?"

Do I want to know what she thinks? *Always*. All the time. Yes, I want to know what she thinks, about everything.

"Yeah," I say. "Please share."

"I think you should keep trying. They're going to realize they're wrong. Or just do it anyway, outside of school."

"Like, our own thing?"

"Yeah," she says. "Screw the school, you don't need them. I mean, like . . . you don't need anyone else to do this."

"Thanks, Brooklyn," I say, feeling weirdly touched.

"Seriously, I think it's really cool that you're trying to do this," Brooklyn says. "I wish a league like that existed now."

She leans in slightly, so that our shoulders are touching. "If you started one, I'd join."

I almost can't breathe. "You would?"

"Yeah," she says. "I would."

We're just looking at each other, sitting close, and I'm hardly daring to breathe.

The slam of a locker door, from somewhere down the hall, makes us both jump and move slightly apart.

Suddenly I realize she's been sitting with me on this bench for kind of a long time.

"Hey, shouldn't you be in class right now?"

"I have a spare," she says. "But — shouldn't you?"

"Oh, yeah," I say. "Probably."

Reluctantly, I get up . . . and, I think, she seems a little slow to get up too. Does she also wish that we could stay sitting here, talking, for a little bit longer? Or am I just imagining that?

"I'll see you in German, later?"

"Yeah," I say, smiling. "See you later. And, uh, thanks for listening."

"No worries," she says, smiling back. "I like talking to you, you know."

She heads off down the hall, looking completely casual. I walk back to class but my heart is racing. The rest of the day, I can't stop thinking about our conversation, and sitting on the bench with Brooklyn, leaning in to each other. I replay it all in my head, over and over.

* * *

I talk about it with Skye. Later that week, we stop by Ms. Arsenault's classroom again.

She looks up at us expectantly. "Well?"

I glance at Skye for support, and she nods.

"We want to keep going," I say. "With *our* name."

Ms. Arsenault smiles and nods. "Very good."

* * *

Skye comes over to my house after school one day. On the floor of my room, we look up places with gyms that we could rent near us. We decide to try and make it a place in London, to be more central if people are coming from around the city. The actual City of London rents recreation spaces, and so do the Boys and Girls Club of London. Boler Mountain rents their outdoor beach volleyball courts — it's been a warm autumn, but as soon as the snow falls we won't be able to play there. We can also rent space from Summit Sports at the ActivityPlex, which has almost brand new courts.

Once we have a list of places, Skye and I split it up, each taking half. We email each place, asking how much it costs to rent the space for an hour or two on a weeknight.

"Do we even have money to rent space?" Skye asks me.

I shrug. "I don't know. That's step two."

First, you figure out what you want to do — *then* you find a way to make it happen.

We hear back from most places within a few days. A couple places don't get back, even with a follow-up email. Neither Skye or I want to call — the idea of making a phone call makes us want to die — so I beg my mom and she calls for us, rolling her eyes but getting the info we need.

Finally, we have all the rates for each place on our list. The ActivityPlex — which I was hoping for — is gorgeous, but turns out to be insanely expensive to rent. The cheapest and best space overall is the YMCA in central London, for just $90/hour. And they have availability on Thursday nights, the day we want to run the league.

At lunch, Skye and I discuss how we're going to come up with $90 every week.

"We could charge people? You know, like five dollars at the door?"

"But what if we don't get enough people? Also, we'd need, like, nearly twenty people to come, to get up to $90."

"You'd need eighteen people," Alexis, who's sitting with us, says.

"Right. What if we don't get that many?" I say.

"Could we get someone else to pay it?" Skye asks.

"Who, our parents?" I say.

"No, like a business or something. You know how they'll buy jerseys for soccer teams and stuff? We could do that."

"But we're not going to have jerseys," I say.

"I mean, not right now, but we could someday!" Skye says. "That's not the point, though. Maybe they'd just agree to cover the cost as, like, a community donation."

"You just have to find the gayest business in London to ask," Alexis says.

"Lush?" Skye suggests.

Alexis and I both burst out laughing. That's the gay nightclub in London.

"I don't think we're even allowed *in* there, Skye, so I don't think they're going to sponsor a teen volleyball league," I say, laughing.

"Subaru?" Alexis says. I know she's making a joke, and kind of a mean one, but actually . . .

"The London Subaru dealership *does* fly a pride flag all year round," I say.

"How do you know that?"

"My dentist is in south London," I say. "We drive by it."

"Okay. So we could ask Subaru," Skye says. "Or, like,

another gay business. Or just a business that has a pride flag, or a little gay sticker in their window, or whatever."

"And if they all say no?" I ask.

"If they all say no . . ." Skye says. "Start a GoFundMe page? Or . . . I did save most of my tips from the coffee truck this summer. And that could get us through, I don't know, the first five weeks?"

"Skye!" I say. "No. You can't give up all your tips for this stupid volleyball league."

"It's not stupid," Skye says. "I think it's actually a very non-stupid way to spend my money."

We stare at each other for a moment. I can't believe she'd do that for this league.

Alexis clears her throat. "I'd also be willing to pitch in."

My head swivels from Skye to her. "You would?"

"Sure," she says, shrugging. "My gran gave me, like, $200 for my birthday last month. You guys could have it, if you want. I mean, it's your guys' thing, and I want to . . . you know . . . support it."

I don't know what to say.

"Oh my god, don't cry!" Alexis says, sounding alarmed.

"I'm not!" I say, but then I realize that my eyes are wet. I reach up and quickly swipe at them. "Sorry. I'm not."

I reach across the table, on an impulse, holding my hands

out. Skye and Alexis each take one, and then they reach out and hold each other's spare hand, forming a triangle. For a moment, we just sit there like that, connected.

Then I clear my throat and gently take my hands back.

"Okay," I say. "So . . . we could try and get a sponsor . . . or do like a crowdfunding thing . . . and as a backup, we have . . . we have funds for the first weeks."

"Either way, we could do this," Skye says, meeting my eyes. "We don't need the school."

"We can do this," I say, smiling and nodding.

* * *

Skye and I go to the main office the next day at lunch.

"Hi," I say to the secretary. "We're here to see Mr. Stapleton. Is he in?"

"I think he's on lunch. I can check— "

"Mackenzie!"

At my name, we turn and see Mr. Stapleton leaning out of his office. He waves us in.

We go in and take a seat in front of his desk.

"I was just about to go for lunch when I heard you asking for me," he says. He smiles at us, acting friendly. "I've been waiting to hear what you wanted to do for the volleyball league, ever since we talked about it. This *is* about the league, right?"

"Yes," I say, "it's about the league."

"Fantastic! So," he says, "have you decided what you're going to call the club?"

Skye and I glance at each other, then back at him.

"Actually," Skye says, "we've decided not to run it here."

"Oh," Mr. Stapleton says. His face flickers, and he looks just a little disappointed — but also, maybe, a little relieved? "That's too bad. It was a nice idea. But I understand, it's hard to commit to starting a league, and it takes a lot of time."

"No, we're still running it," I say. "We've actually found a local gym space to rent. It's not part of the school. It won't be a school club. But we're starting it anyway."

"I don't . . . I'm not sure what you're trying to say, here, girls."

"We didn't want to change the name," Skye says. "It's the Gays and Slays Volleyball League, and that's what we're calling it. And if the school doesn't want to support that, we didn't want to run some pseudo-inclusive club."

Mr. Stapleton literally freezes. He just stares from Skye to me, and back to Skye, his face turning slowly red.

Finally, he says, "I . . . I see."

"Okay," Skye says. We stand up. "So, you can just, I don't know, throw away our club application?"

"Actually, I have it," I tell Skye. "He gave it back."

"Perfect," Skye says.

He opens his mouth like he's about to say something, but he doesn't. We don't stick around — I feel like we're treading right on the edge of getting in trouble, so we leave his office, walking back through the main office and trying not to burst out laughing. In the main office, we pass the secretaries, our school principal, Mr. Ramirez, and the other vice principal, Ms. Kaur. They're all standing around the secretary's desk, watching us with their mouths agape.

Crap. Did they just hear us?

Okay, now we *really* might be on the verge of trouble. Meeting Skye's eyes, I can tell she's thinking the exact same thing that I am. We walk out of the office, nobody saying a word, and as soon as we get out of sight, we start running.

We don't stop until we reach a stairwell on the other side of the school, and then we double over, laughing.

"Oh my god!" Skye says. "I can't believe we just did that!"

"Me neither," I say, grinning from ear to ear. "Did you see his face, though?"

"It's a good thing we don't need to borrow their gym," Skye says. "Because they *definitely* wouldn't let us use it now."

"Nope," I say. "But god, that was fun."

CHAPTER SEVEN

Kaffee und Kuchen

"All right, everyone come to the back — in an orderly fashion — to grab your *kaffee und kuchen*," Ms. Martin says. "The movie will start in five minutes."

Brooklyn and I immediately get up and join the line for food. This is the best part of German class: once a week, for the last half of class on Friday, Ms. Martin lets us do something called "*kaffee und kuchen*." She provides coffee, hot chocolate, and tea, and each of us takes a turn bringing in some form of baked good (bonus points if it's German-inspired). Then we sit, turn off the lights, and watch an episode of this insane TV show that was created to accompany our German textbook.

Except that the textbook and TV show were both created in the nineties, and the characters are always having *the most* dramatic stuff happen. And it's always set to the theme of whatever the week's unit is — last week, for example, we learned how to talk about our hobbies and interests, so in the episode, we watched Sabine break up with her boyfriend because he couldn't fix his bicycle and didn't want to try rollerblading with her. She ran off with a new guy, who enjoyed windsurfing, cooking, and skiing.

It's wild and completely hilarious. Sitting in the dark, eating snacks, and giggling with Brooklyn over the hilarious show has become my favourite part of the week.

In the past month, sharing a desk, I've learned a lot more about Brooklyn. I've learned that she's an only child. The green car that she sometimes drives belongs to her mom, an Environmental Officer who works some days at home and some days in the office. Brooklyn gets to borrow it when her mom works from home. Brooklyn is even funnier than I thought she was. Sometimes in class, when we're supposed to be listening to Ms. Martin, or someone is answering a question, Brooklyn will make little comments under her breath to me, and I have to hide my laughter.

I've learned that Brooklyn has a first-period spare because the summer before last, she took an extra-credit phys. ed. course over the summer, which she says was basically like going to the gym every day. She and her dad shoot hoops together almost every day after school. She wants to get a tattoo once she's eighteen, probably more than one.

She doesn't like to read, but she still always comes with her chapter readings done, unlike me, who never does them. Since we're at different levels, we're often split up for discussion times, but sometimes we're left together, and she never gets mad at my terrible German. Instead we just joke about it and she helps me practice.

Now, Brooklyn grabs two hot chocolates, and I take two pieces of Black Forest cake for us.

We've just sat down and picked up our forks when I hear my name being called. We both pause and look up.

Ms. Martin is standing by the class phone, just setting it back down.

"Mackenzie," she says again, beckoning me over.

Oh, no. Am I about to get in trouble for something?

"The office just called," Ms. Martin says. "They'd like you to go down and see Mr. Stapleton, please. Leave your things — they said it wouldn't take too long."

My heart thumping, I head to the office. I don't know exactly why Mr. Stapleton wants to see me, but I have a very strong feeling it has to do with the league — and what Skye and I said to him yesterday.

When I get there, the secretary tells me to go right into Mr.

Stapleton's office. I feel so nervous I think I'm about to pass out.

In his office, I find Mr. Stapleton sitting at his desk, smiling and chatting with Ms. Arsenault, who is sitting in the chair across from him.

"Mackenzie! Please, come in, have a seat," he says.

I sit down beside Ms. Arsenault, giving her a confused glance. She beams back at me.

Okay, *what* is going on?

"Okay, Mackenzie, thanks for coming down," Mr. Stapleton says, folding his hands in front of him on the desk. "We're just waiting for — ah! Skye, come on in."

Skye's just entered, only a few seconds behind me, and looking equally confused. She gives me a look as if to say, *What the heck is going on?* I can only shrug back. I have no idea.

Skye sits down in the last available chair, beside mine, and we both look at Mr. Stapleton expectantly.

"Thanks for coming down, you two," Mr. Stapleton says. "You've probably guessed that this is about the inclusive volleyball league you asked to start. Look, I found it really inspiring, what you said yesterday, and I had some conversations with the principal and our other vice principal, and the school would be happy to approve your club with its original name."

Oh my god.

"And," he continues, "I want to reiterate that the values of the school — diversity, equality, making a place for everyone — those are behind you both. I think this is a great club. I'm sorry we had to go through these workarounds, but I'm really excited to see the club take place."

I can't believe what he's saying. After the last couple meetings we had with him, what he's saying now feels too good to be true.

"So we can call it . . . the Gays and Slays Volleyball League?"

"Yes," he says. "You can. And I think it's going to be a great option for our students to join."

Our students. Wait a minute. I'm suddenly realizing that Skye and I may have forgotten to put something really important on the original form.

"Um . . ." I hesitate, wondering if I should say anything. And then I decide that I should. It's better to be honest now and get to move forward knowing that we're in the clear, than to pretend to be something we're not and have trouble later. "We actually, uh . . . we wanted it to be open to any teens in the area, not just the kids in our school."

"Oh," he says, and sort of pauses. "Okay . . . sorry, I was under the impression that this club was just for our school, as most clubs are."

"I guess it could be, but we were hoping to open it up," I

say. "I mean . . . I don't know if there's enough students who would come out from just our school. And there's not another league like this right now in our area. I think everyone should get a chance to play."

"Okay," Mr. Stapleton says. He's quiet for a minute, nodding, thinking to himself. "Okay. Unfortunately, we aren't allowed to host a club here that's open to all of the schools in the area. It can only really be for our school, which again, we would be happy to support. It just has to stay within our student body."

"Oh."

I feel my heart sink. I should have known. Too good to be true.

"But," Mr. Stapleton says, "if you did want to open it up more, we do rent out the gymnasium, after hours, to local organizations."

"Okay . . ."

"So if you wanted to rent it separately from the school and run the club, that could be an option. Then there are no limits — you can make it open to any teens who are in the area, whether or not they go to this school, or even this school board. And I think we could give you the subsidized rate, that we give to non-profits and certain other groups."

"Okay . . ." I say. "How much would that be?"

"It's nothing," he says. "$0/hour. You would rent it for free."

Suddenly the sinking feeling is gone. Skye and I meet each other's eyes. That means that we don't have to get a sponsor. Skye doesn't have to give up her tip money, and Alexis doesn't have to give up her birthday money. I feel myself starting to smile, and Skye is smiling too.

"I think that could work," I say.

"But you have to understand, if you're doing it this way, it's not going to be run with the school anymore. It would be like the school was sponsoring it, but we're not legally responsible for things anymore. We can still promote it here and support it, but it would be your own thing. Are you okay with that?"

Our own thing. With the freedom to do what we want with it.

I look at Skye, who gives me one quick, decisive nod.

"We're okay with that," I say, grinning.

* * *

In the hallway, Skye and I start jumping up and down.

"Oh my god! *Oh my god!*" Skye says.

"I know, right?"

"This slaps," Skye says. "I can't believe this."

"Right?" I say. "Let's celebrate after school. I've got to get back to class."

I'm so excited about the league. But most of all, right now, I want to run and tell Brooklyn the news.

Skye and I hug, and then I practically run back to class, I'm so stoked.

When I get back, they're partway through the latest episode. I sneak back to my desk in the darkness, trying not to block anyone's view.

Brooklyn is watching the show, chewing her lip, both pieces of cake still sitting untouched on our desks. When she sees me, she instantly sits up straighter and leans over.

"What happened?" she asks, in a hushed whisper, as I sit back down beside her. "Was it about the league? Did you get in trouble?"

"Yeah, it was about the league," I whisper back. "But we didn't get in trouble. Kind of the opposite . . ."

Bending our heads close together, talking as quietly as I can under the sounds of the German TV show, I tell her all about it.

CHAPTER EIGHT

Setting Up

"You girls have everything you need?" Mom asks.

"I think so, yeah," I say.

I glance at Skye in the back seat, and she gives me a thumbs-up. My mom is driving us to downtown London. We're going to hang up posters for the inclusive volleyball league. The first date for the club is set — we're starting in two weeks.

Mom printed the posters for me, and Skye and I are armed with twenty copies, plus tape and a stapler.

Mom drops us off at the Black Walnut. We figured we'd start here.

"Be safe!" she calls, as we climb out. "Call me when you're done!"

We wave goodbye and head into the café. Inside, there's

people sitting at the little tables and chatting. The smell of coffee and baked goods is irresistible. Immediately to the left of the entrance, they have a large bulletin board, with posters about almost everything: dog-sitting services, the latest musical at the Grand Theatre, an upcoming fundraising event at a brewery . . .

"Do you think we can just put it up, or should we ask?" Skye says.

I look at the board, then at the front counter. "Let's ask, I guess?"

There's a short line-up, and we wait beside the cases of pastry and quiche. Skye's trying not to drool over the cruffins, but I can barely focus.

I'm *terrified.*

I didn't expect to feel like this, but I am. Hanging up posters for the league around town seemed like a good idea. But now, holding out posters and tape, I'm suddenly gripped by a quiet fear. What if they say no? What if they say that, despite the number of posters already up, they don't want ours? What if they're just weirdly homophobic about it? What do I do then? How do I react? What if people stare?

When we get up to the cashier, I nearly lose my voice.

"Hi, uh, um, we were . . ." I say, stammering. I force myself to take a deep breath. "We were wondering if we could, um . . ."

Skye jumps in — thank god for her.

"We were wondering if we could hang our poster on your board?" she asks, brightly. She holds up one of the posters so that they can see. It's got all the info on it — date, time, location in Medway's gymnasium — and a volleyball, bouncing across the top, with an illustrated rainbow stretching behind it.

"Oh my gosh, of course!" the cashier says. "I love that! Can I see . . ."

She peers at the poster, reading it:

GAYS AND SLAYS VOLLEYBALL LEAGUE
For 2SLGBTQIA+ youth and allies
Join us for a fun game each week
in a safe, inclusive & accepting space
Ages 13–17
All welcome

"That's fantastic!" she says. "Yes, of course, you can hang your poster! Do you mind if I snap a photo? I'm going to tell my son about it, too."

"Oh — go for it!" I say. In a second, all of my fear has disappeared. I'm feeling so relieved.

She takes a photo and then tells us to put it up "wherever we can find space."

"There're pushpins on the board," she says.

We find a prime spot and put it up, stepping back to admire our handiwork. Seeing the poster here, out in the real world, I can't help but feel weirdly proud. I take a photo of the poster myself, and so does Skye.

We speak at the same time:

"Ready for the next place?" I ask.

"Want to get cruffins?" Skye asks.

Obviously, yes. We get a cruffin each (Skye gets lavender cream; I get maple custard) and iced coffees. After quickly scarfing down our baked goods, we head out and continue on our mission.

We work our way down Richmond Row, heading south. We stop in any shop that we can see displaying community posters already (we've decided not to waste time asking places if they don't look like they let people put up posters). Every time we walk into a new place and ask if we can hang our poster, I experience the same quiet fear as I did the first time. But Skye is right beside me, and she jumps in whenever I falter.

Every single place we ask says "yes." It fills my spirit. It makes it a little bit easier to ask at the next place.

We hit up Banh Mi Express and the bubble tea place, Presotea. We make a quick detour down Piccadilly to hang a poster in the window of Haven's Creamery. We walk past all the bars, Ceeps and Jack Astor's and El Furniture Warehouse, and talk about how we can't wait to be in uni or college and go to places like these. When we get to Dundas, we loop around and put a poster in the board game café, Saga.

We duck into the Covent Garden Market and get lost, like, five times, trying to find who we can ask about hanging the poster. Finally we find a tiny office in the back. The clerk instantly gives our posters a stamp of approval (it's a literal stamp) and we get to hang it up on their giant wall of posters. A couple of the market vendors notice what we're doing and offer to hang a copy at their stalls, too.

We put two up in the weird building that houses the library, that feels like a mall but is mostly office space. We get one in Attic Books, one in a custom dessert shop, and another in the thrift store on Dundas.

Everyone is so nice — they all say yes. Only one worker says that they have to ask their manager, but then lets us hang the poster up, anyway, pending approval. There's about a dozen other posters hanging up in their window — she can't imagine it will be an issue.

We run out of posters sooner than I imagine. I call my mom, who says she'll pick us up outside of the market, and we start walking back along Dundas to meet her. We're doubling back now on our route from this morning and going past the same shops we went by earlier. At all the places we hung up posters, I find myself seeking ours out. I feel this insane rush of joy whenever I see one of our posters hanging in a window.

"That went *so* well," I say.

"I know, right?" Skye says. "I love that everyone said yes."

"I know! That was so— "

I stop midsentence. I'm looking across the street, at one of the dessert shops where we hung a poster just an hour ago. It was the one where the worker said she had to get her manager's approval, but we hung it up anyway. The poster is gone now.

"Look," I say. Skye follows my gaze and frowns.

"Didn't we . . . I thought we gave them a poster?"

"We did," I say. "It was right there."

"All of the other posters are still there," Skye says slowly.

"I know."

"So . . . the manager must have taken it down?"

"Yeah."

"I guess it wasn't approved."

It wasn't approved, but every other poster in the window was? About the fundraising events and lost dogs and apartments for rent?

Only our poster, with its bouncing volleyball and bright rainbow, is gone.

"Do you want to go in and ask them about it?" Skye asks. "We could confront them. Ask them why they took it down . . ."

I think about it for a moment, but the answer is no.

Today has been such a good day. If I go in there, and they say something hurtful, I'm probably going to cry.

I just want to keep today as a good day.

"No," I say, shaking my head. "Not today."

"That's okay," Skye says. She reaches over and loops her arm in mine. "Hey — I don't think I've said this yet — but I think you're incredibly brave for doing this. And I know that all of this has probably got to be harder for you than it is for me."

"Thanks, Skye," I say. I rest my head on her shoulder and let myself feel loved.

"We hung up a lot of posters," Skye reminds me.

"Yeah," I say. "I'm proud of us. Thanks for doing this with me."

"Of course, girlie," Skye says. "Should we go find your mom?"

"Yeah," I say. "Let's go."

CHAPTER NINE

First Night

The first night of the league, I'm literally buzzing with excitement.

I head home after school, because the league doesn't start until 7:00 p.m. (I wanted to hold it right after school, but Skye pointed out that if we want people from other schools to come, we have to give them time to get here). At home, I'm way too anxious. I annoy everyone until Grace finally just offers to give me a ride to the gym early.

She drops me off at 6:00 p.m. I get into the gymnasium and start setting things up. We borrowed a few volleyballs from my family's stash of sports equipment, and the school's letting us use their nets.

I'm terrified that nobody will show up. But Skye is going to be here, obviously. Ms. Arsenault will be here — even though we're not a school club anymore, she's agreed to stay involved as a chaperone/supervisor for the league.

Brooklyn said that she would come, too. My heart skips a beat every time I think about her. I'm so excited, thinking about her showing up. Even if nobody else comes out tonight, it will be worth all of this, just to hang out with her.

Skye gets here at 6:30 and helps me finish setting up the nets. Ms. Arsenault gets here at 6:50.

At 7:00 p.m., taking a deep breath, I walk over and check that the door is unlocked.

It's open. Nobody is here.

At 7:05, there's still nobody here.

Ms. Arsenault reminds us that it's just the first week, and it may take a while to "build momentum."

I check my phone about every ten seconds. I don't get it. Brooklyn said she would come. Why would she bail? I thought we were vibing in class, and our conversation on the bench — but maybe I was misreading things. Maybe she doesn't really like me?

"Hey, let's toss the ball around," Skye says, trying to cheer me up.

Slowly, I get to my feet. We bump it back and forth for a bit. If nothing else, it keeps me from checking my phone nonstop.

At 7:10, we hear the door creak open. All three of us whip around to watch it. Skye misses the ball coming back to her and lets it bounce away.

It's not Brooklyn.

It's a skinny guy with brown hair, stepping through. He glances from me to Skye to Ms. Arsenault.

"Is this the . . . the inclusive volleyball league?"

"Yes! Yes, it is!" Ms. Arsenault says. "Come on in. I'm Katie Arsenault. This is Mackenzie and Skye."

"Hi," I say. I'm trying to hide my disappointment that he's not Brooklyn.

He's a person who showed up. And that's still good.

"I'm Trevor," he says.

"We're happy you're here, Trevor," Ms. Arsenault says. "Come on in."

We chat for a minute and learn that he's from a high school in Central London — his mom, as it turns out, is the cashier from Black Walnut.

We get a game going, even though there's only four of us. Ms. Arsenault — who I know wasn't planning to play — jumps in so that we can play two vs. two. Trevor and I play together, with Skye and Ms. Arsenault on the other side.

Trevor actually turns out to be very nice, and *very* good. We beat the other two so badly in the first set that Skye demands we're put on different teams to level the playing field. We switch to me and Skye against Trevor and Ms. Arsenault, and the game becomes a more even match. As we play, everyone relaxes a little, and we start joking around between serves.

Throughout the night, I keep glancing at the door, hoping that Brooklyn will show up at the last minute. But she never does.

We wrap things up at 8:00 p.m.

Skye and I start taking down the nets. We set up four nets and only needed one, in the end. It's hard not to feel a little defeated by that. I hate the thought of having to take down all four now.

But then I realize that Trevor hasn't left — he's helping Ms. Arsenault take down one of the other nets. So we don't have to take them all down ourselves, after all.

When everything's put away, we all grab our water bottles and start walking out together.

"Thanks for organizing," Trevor says, to all of us.

"Oh, you're so welcome!" Ms. Arsenault says. "Thank you for joining us tonight. Do you play a lot?"

"I used to," he says. "I stopped two years ago."

He pauses, as if deciding whether to say more, and then adds: "I quit in middle school, after one of my teammates wouldn't stop calling me homophobic slurs at practices. Never when the coach was around, or other teammates."

Damn.

"I'm really sorry you had to go through that," Ms. Arsenault says.

"Thanks. It was hard when it happened, but it was really nice to play tonight. Is there going to be a game again next week?"

Ms. Arsenault glances over at me. I clear my throat.

"Yes," I say. "Same time, same place. We'll see you next week?"

"I'll be here," he says. Smiling, he waves goodbye.

Ms. Arsenault tells us goodnight and heads off as well. Skye reaches over and squeezes my shoulder.

"How ya feeling?"

"Crappy," I admit. "I just thought . . . more people would come."

"One did," Skye reminds me. "And that's still a win."

"Yeah," I say. "I know."

And I *do* know that she's right. But I still go home feeling crushed. Partly because only one person came to our league. But mostly because of the fact that Brooklyn never showed.

CHAPTER TEN

Brooklyn Bailed

I manage to stop myself from texting her. That would feel too pathetic. But it's hard. All I want to do is message her and ask, *Where were you? You said you'd be there.*

She doesn't text me, either. I can't imagine how I'm going to get through the whole school day before I get to see her in fourth period.

Luckily, I don't have to wait that long. When I get to school that morning, first thing, Brooklyn is waiting beside my locker.

"Hey," she says. "How did it go last night?"

How did it go last night? Is she serious? How can she bail, and then ask me like that — like she cares?

"Uh," I say. "Fine."

I can't meet her eyes. I focus on opening my locker, and

sorting through my bag, putting away the things that I won't need for the morning. There are other students in the hall, chatting with friends, and a few other people at their lockers.

"Just . . . fine?" Brooklyn asks. I can tell she wants to hear more; she wants me to tell her all about it. But if she's so fucking interested, why wasn't she there?

"It was great," I snap. "Okay? Best night ever."

"Hey, Mackenzie . . ." Brooklyn reaches out and gently rests her fingertips on my arm. I stop rummaging through my bag. "I'm sorry I didn't come last night. Are you mad?"

"No, I'm not, I'm just . . ." I glance over at her and sigh. On my arm, where she's touching me, it feels like my whole body is on fire. I can't think straight anymore (literally). "I was just . . . disappointed not to see you there."

"I know," Brooklyn says, softly. "I'm sorry I wasn't there. I said I would be, and I wasn't."

"Why weren't you, then?" I ask, raising my eyes to meet hers.

"I had basketball tryouts for the girl's rep team," she says. "It was supposed to be earlier in the evening, but then they bumped the time at the last minute, and I went to those. I thought I could still do both — I was trying to get to your league — that's why I didn't text you. But then they made us do, like, an hour of drills and another hour playing a friendly game, and by the time it was done, it was too late, and my phone was dead, so I couldn't even text you. I'm sorry."

"Oh," I say. I know how important basketball is to her, and I get prioritizing a tryout. It's not like you get a second chance for those. "Okay."

"So . . . you're not mad?"

"No," I say. "I mean, I get it. It's okay that you prioritized it. I wish you'd told me that the girl's rep tryouts were that night, though. I could have moved the inclusive league to a different day or something."

"You'd have moved it just for me?" Brooklyn says. She smiles a little, and tips her head to the side. "You really wanted me there, huh?"

I feel myself blushing. Her hand is still on my arm.

"Yeah, I mean . . . just to bring up the overall athleticism in the league," I say. "You know, you're so . . . fit."

"Thanks," Brooklyn says. She's still smiling, her eyes on mine.

Our moment is interrupted by the bell. Her hand goes back to her side.

Goddammit.

"I've got to go, but I really am sorry about last night, okay?"

"It's okay. Don't worry about it."

"And I'm going to make it to the league next time. Just so long as it's not scheduled for my basketball practice days."

"Mm-hmm," I say, pretending to think. "Okay, and what days are those?"

"Every Monday and Wednesday," she says. She takes a few steps backwards, starting to walk away. The hallway is busy, with students going in every direction towards their first class.

"I'll try to remember that," I say. She laughs and disappears into the crowd.

CHAPTER ELEVEN

One on One

Over the next week, we really amp up our efforts to share the news of the league.

Skye makes us an Insta account for the league. A few of our posts get shared by other London groups, and people start tagging each other in the comments. It doesn't go viral or anything, but every comment gives me hope.

On Saturday, Brooklyn comes over to mine. Sitting together in the family room, I teach her how to use a design program, Canva. It's what I used to make the poster and it's super easy. Together, we design a four-by-six-inch postcard that we're going to print and give to friends to hand out. We also design some more graphics for Skye to put on socials. I don't technically *need* Brooklyn's help for this — I could have done it myself — but it's honestly really helpful to have a second set of eyes when I'm second-guessing a font choice or what looks good. And obviously, it's more fun to do it together.

We're almost done when my parents walk by, on their way out the door with Grace.

"We're leaving now, honey," my mom says, waving. "You guys can order food for dinner, if you like, or we can bring you something after the game."

"Okay, thanks," I say.

Mom hesitates. She's clearly trying to figure out if Brooklyn is just a new friend, or whether she's maybe-more-than-a-friend? She settles with a simple, "It was nice to meet you, Brooklyn."

"Thanks, you too, Mrs. Wilson."

Grace — who has her headphones on and is already trying to get in the focus zone for her soccer game — just waves, and they head out.

We're alone in the house now. Tommy is at a friend's house tonight, and Noah obviously is at uni. He's only an hour away, but he usually just comes home for holidays and long weekends.

We finish working on our design, and then order pizza.

"Okay, it says it's going to be thirty minutes," I say, closing the laptop.

"Good, I'm starving," Brooklyn says. "So, uh . . . what do you want to do while we wait?"

Everything she says sends fire through my whole body.

"Um . . . whatever you want. I'm easy."

She glances out the window, then gives me a sly glance. "I noticed you have a hoop in your driveway."

I can't help but laugh. "It's Noah's, mostly. My oldest brother."

"You play at all?"

"I mean, a little," I say. "You want to shoot some hoops?"

"Yeah," she says. "Let's do it."

I grab the ball, we lace up our shoes, and head out.

We warm up with a couple games of H-O-R-S-E. Then we switch to a game of one-on-one.

Brooklyn gets the first point, but I get the second and third. I suspect she's going easy on me until she gets five more baskets in a row. She doesn't miss a shot.

We cover each other closely as we play. Brooklyn's got good defense — she's not afraid to get up in my space. I match it, getting just as close to her. As we play, our arms touch, our shoulders and hips nudge each other. I get so close that her blond hair brushes my shoulder, and I can smell her shampoo. It smells like turmeric and honey.

We get up to twenty-four (Brooklyn) to ten (me, sadly)

when a car pulls up. It's our food.

We grab it from the driver and decide to stay outside to eat, even though it's almost dark. It's so warm out and we're both hot now from playing. We sit on the driveway under the hoop, the pizza box between us, eating without plates. Brooklyn keeps her hand on the basketball as we eat, rolling it gently back and forth on the ground as she eats, holding her pizza slice with her other hand.

Even here, sitting on the ground and eating pizza, she's gorgeous. She's wearing a loose mauve shirt, her hair hanging down, and she looks absolutely stunning.

"Your parents — are they watching Grace's game tonight?" Brooklyn asks.

I realize I've been staring and try to pull myself out of it. "Uh, yeah. Yeah, they are."

"Would you normally go watch her game, too? Or are you staying in tonight just to hang with me?"

"Actually, I hardly ever see Grace's games," I admit. "Normally I'd have practice or one of my own games, but . . . not anymore."

Brooklyn nods, sympathetically. "Is it hard, not playing?"

"A bit," I say. "But also, you know, not. I don't know if you heard . . . do you know why I'm not playing this year?"

Brooklyn shakes her head. "Not really. Just that you didn't

get along with the other girls on the team, or something?"

"Huh," I say. "Yeah. I guess you could say that."

Brooklyn keeps slowly rolling the ball back and forth on the ground, but she doesn't say anything. She's quiet, listening, waiting while I find the right words.

"I came out last year," I tell her. "It wasn't a huge deal, really. But afterwards, a bunch of little stuff changed between me and my teammates. And it was so weird because I've played with most of these girls for, like, two years or more. But I felt like . . . they didn't trust me, anymore, or want to hang out with me, or want me there."

Brooklyn nods, her eyes on mine.

"We used to hang out all the time outside of practice and games. Like, after practice we'd sit in the parking lot, or all go for iced coffee together . . . just random stuff, you know? And it was sort of an unwritten rule that everyone was invited, but people stopped asking if I was coming with them. And one time, I joined, and everyone acted really surprised. It hit this weird point where I was never sure if I was actually invited or not, so I stopped going. And then they had a sleepover and actually didn't invite me — like, they on purpose did not invite me. And I got really fed up with it. They were supposed to be my teammates, you know? And I knew that when I came out, some things would change. It just . . . it really surprised me that out of everybody, they were the ones who handled it the worst."

My throat's started to close up, and I realize with a shock that my eyes are wet.

"Sorry, um . . . I didn't mean to go on like that . . ."

"Hey, it's okay," Brooklyn says, softly. She lets go of the basketball, letting it roll away, and reaches out to take my hands. "That sounds like it was really hard."

"Yeah," I say. "It was. And even now, like, I decided not to try out this year and nobody on the team, aside from Alexis, has reached out, or asked why I'm not playing, or been like, 'Hey, we miss you!' It's just like they've forgotten me. They don't care."

"It's too bad you weren't into basketball," Brooklyn says. "About half the girls on that team are gay."

She's trying to cheer me up, and it works. I can't help but laugh a little at that.

"Too bad," I say. "I could have fit right in."

"No doubt," she says, grinning. "Although it would be hard for me."

"For you? Why?"

"You'd be such a distraction on the court."

I laugh again. "A distraction on the court? Really? Because you had no problem kicking my ass tonight."

She laughs, too. She's still holding my hands, running her thumbs gently along the tops of mine.

"Is that why you wanted to start the inclusive league?" Brooklyn asks. "Because of everything with your teammates?"

"Yeah," I say. "Exactly. It's personal for me, you know? Because I really just want to play. But I needed . . . a different space, I guess."

"It's really cool that you're doing this."

"I'm trying to, anyway. I just hope more people show up, so we can actually get a game going without Ms. Arsenault having to play."

"Yeah," Brooklyn says.

Her phone buzzes, and she takes a hand away to check it.

"It's my mom," she says, looking at the screen. "Sorry, I've got to go . . ."

We climb to our feet. Brooklyn squeezes my hand before letting go.

"Hey, what are you doing tomorrow?" she asks.

"Not much. I was going to hang out with Skye. Why?"

"Do you have any more of those posters? You said you hung some up downtown and on Richmond . . ."

"Yeah, I can get more."

"Do you want to go hang more up tomorrow? To help spread the word? I can drive us. Skye can come, too. I was thinking we could hit up some more areas around the city — maybe go to Wortley, some libraries . . . just share it everywhere."

"Oh, wow," I say. "Um . . . that would be cool. I'll text Skye, see if that works for her, but . . . yeah. That would be great."

"Okay. Cool," Brooklyn says. "I'll see you tomorrow, then."

"See you tomorrow."

Smiling, Brooklyn bends down to pick up the basketball. She tosses it to me before heading to her car parked on the street at the end of my driveway.

* * *

Skye gets dropped off at my house on Sunday morning, and I fill her in on the plan.

"Is that okay with you?" I ask. "If Brooklyn comes? She can drive us."

"Yeah, of course," Skye says. "I'm excited to get to know her. So . . . are you two, like, a thing?"

"I don't know," I say. "I think . . . I might be in a situationship?"

"Meaning?"

"I'm super into her. I don't know if she's into me," I say.

"She's driving us around to help you hang posters for your gay volleyball league," Skye says, rolling her eyes. "I think she *might* be into you."

Brooklyn comes to pick us up thirty minutes later. After a quick discussion, we decide on our plan for the day.

We plan to drive in a sort of clockwise direction, hitting up east London, south London, and then west London. Along the way we stop at all the libraries, thrift stores, and cafés that we can think of.

Driving around with Brooklyn and Skye turns out to be really fun. Skye lets me sit shotgun and leans forward between our seats to chat as we drive. Brooklyn and Skye get along easily and we don't run out of things to talk about — or laugh about — all day.

Our last stop is Wortley Village. We park across from the YMCA and get out to walk around. We put posters in Plant Matter Kitchen, the hardware store, and Mai's Café & Bistro. The Old South Village Pub lets us put it up prominently on their hostess stand. Sidetrack asks if they can have more than one, so that they give a couple to their friends, and we happily give them five copies.

We're discussing if we want to try driving out to Komoka and Kilworth and hang posters up there when we realize we're out of posters. Deciding to call it a day, we head home. We stop for iced coffees on the way back to my house, drinking them in the car as we go back up Richmond. Brooklyn buys us all coffee.

“Thanks for driving us,” I say to Brooklyn. She looks so cool, even when she’s driving. I don’t even have my G1 yet, but I know I’m going to be a bucket of nerves when I drive. Brooklyn drives with one hand, music playing, window open slightly and blowing her hair back.

“No worries,” Brooklyn says. “It was fun.”

“I hope it works,” Skye says. “If nobody shows up this week, after we hung all those posters, I’m going to lose my mind.”

“I bet Trevor will come back,” I say.

“I’ll be there, too,” Brooklyn says. She smiles over at me, and this moment, driving in the car in the autumn sunshine, iced coffee in my hand, playing music and laughing with Brooklyn and Skye — this moment feels perfect.

CHAPTER TWELVE

Gays and Slays

Grace drops me off the next Thursday with a wave.

"Good luck, Kenz!"

"Thanks," I say. "See ya. Come back in like, two hours?"

"Sure," Grace says. She's going to hang out with some friends tonight. She waves goodbye as she pulls away.

Turning to face the gym, I set my shoulders and take a deep breath before heading in. It's the second week of the league, and I'm trying to approach the whole night differently. No nerves. No hoping people show up. Whoever shows up — however *many* people show up — I'm going to try and be happy about it.

Skye arrives a little after me, and we start setting the nets up together. Ms. Arsenault shows up next. And then — my heart starts beating a mile a minute — Brooklyn walks in.

She reassured me earlier today in class that she'd show up. But it's really good to see her here.

"Go on," Skye says, nodding with her head. "I can finish the nets."

I walk over to greet Brooklyn. "Hey!"

"Hey," she says, smiling. She sets her water bottle down on one of the benches in between the courts and gives me a hug. *Ah!*

"Thanks for coming," I say. I'm trying to contain my excitement. I don't want to seem over-the-top excited that she's here — but I am.

"I'm happy to be here," she says.

Over the next fifteen minutes, a few more people trickle in. Trevor is back, and a few new faces as well. Skye and I greet them as they each come in. Ms. Arsenault gives people volleyballs and they start warming up, volleying or bumping the balls back and forth in pairs or groups of three.

At five minutes past seven, I look around and realize that we have enough people to play four vs. four. Ms. Arsenault doesn't even need to play. I'm about to raise my voice and tell everyone that we can get started when the door opens again.

I'm expecting maybe one more person, already thinking about how we can add them as a sub — how exciting is it, that we have enough people now to play with subs? — but it's not one person. It's five. Meaghan, Olivia, Alexis, Mckenna, and Lucy. All of them are from the girls' volleyball team — the one I left.

I'm almost too stunned to speak, not just by the fact that they've shown up, but also because Alexis is with them. Why wouldn't she have given me the heads-up that they were coming?

Suddenly, everyone is watching them as they walk in. The volleyballs stop flying through the air and the chatter stops as they walk over to where I'm standing. Skye takes a few steps so she's close by.

"Hey," Meaghan says, smiling at me.

"Um, hi," I say.

"We came to play," Meaghan says. "If that's okay? This league is for *everyone*, right?"

What the heck?

I can't help but feel like they're not showing up to be supportive — they're here to make a point. Alexis told me that some of the co-captains, including Meaghan, were pissed when they found out I wasn't just leaving the team, I was starting my own, inclusive league. As if I was saying that they were all homophobic. And now, showing up here, they're trying to prove that they're *not*.

I glance at Skye, but she's shooting dagger eyes at Alexis.

What am I supposed to say? I don't really want them here. The league exists *because* of them, in a way. But if I kick them out without even giving them a chance, isn't that bad? We're supposed to be a space for everyone.

"Um, sure," I say. "We're just warming up. Grab a ball."

"Sure," Meaghan says. Still smiling, the five of them all spread out in a large circle together, and slowly the gym starts to fill with the sounds of volleyball again.

Skye steps over to me and tugs at my arm. "What are you doing?" she whispers.

I turn to huddle with her, so that nobody can see what we're talking about. "I don't know," I whisper back. "I would feel bad kicking them out."

"I wouldn't," Skye says.

"I think we have to give them a chance," I say. "We can't just kick them out, assuming they'll be . . . you know . . ."

"Homophobic jerks?"

"Yeah," I say.

We both glance over our shoulders, taking in our players. People are still laughing, volleying and bumping the ball back and forth, having a good time. My eyes go to Brooklyn, who's passing the ball now with Trevor. She sees me staring and winks at me, quickly, before turning her attention back to her warmup. My stomach flips.

Ms. Arsenault is on the other side of the gym, watching people warm up, too. She catches my eye and raises her eyebrows, then looks pointedly at the volleyball girls. I bite my lip, then shrug.

I turn back to Skye. "Okay, what if we let them stay, but if they do anything bad, they're out?"

"Define 'bad,'" Skye says.

"Like, if they say anything, if they do like . . . I don't know . . . a rude hand gesture, or something. Like, zero tolerance."

"Okay," Skye agrees. "That seems fair. As long as you're cool with it."

I take a deep breath. "I guess so. Let's get started."

We turn back around, and I raise my voice. "Okay! We're gonna get into two teams, everyone, and Skye and I are going to count you off . . ."

We count everyone off by one, two, one, two. I manage to work it out so that I count both myself and Brooklyn on team two.

"Okay! Let's play," I say. "Team one that side, team two, we're this side."

Everyone moves into place. Brooklyn gently bumps into me as we walk.

"Looks like we're playing on the same team, huh?" she says.

"What a coincidence," I joke, and she laughs.

I'm trying to be chill and ignore the nagging feeling in my chest. But ever since the volleyball girls walked in, I can't help but feel like I'm bracing for someone to say something unkind.

A couple of people (including Brooklyn) ask for a reminder of the rules before we start playing, so I give a quick recap. But as soon as we start, the vibes are off. It's nothing like last week. The volleyball girls are playing like we're in finals, not like it's a friendly game. They spike the ball at every chance, elbow their own teammates out of the way, and yell when the ball is coming in. I can see the other players starting to play less, backing off bit by bit, getting scared. This is too intense. It's supposed to be a fun game.

I'm trying to stay calm, but I'm starting to get mad. What are they trying to do? Prove that they're better at volleyball? Why are they *here*?

The game keeps going, getting more and more intense.

And then, midway through the second set, Mckenna dives for the ball at the end of a rally and misses it. Olivia, who's sitting on the sidelines, waiting to go in, cups her hand to her mouth and calls out, in a deep tone, "Gaaaay!"

All of the volleyball girls laugh. But I swear, I can feel everyone else in the room bristle.

That's it. They have to go.

I meet Skye's eyes across the net — she's playing on the

team with Mckenna and Olivia — and nod at her, then I jog quietly off court. Brooklyn is standing on our team's sidelines, waiting to go in, and I ask her, "Sub in for me?"

She's confused, but she reaches out, tapping my hand reflexively and jogging in. I walk over to where Olivia is standing by the wall, getting there at the same time as Skye.

She looks defensively from one of us to the other.

"Hey," I say. The game is continuing behind us, and I don't want to cause a big scene. "Can we talk to you in the hall for a sec?"

"Sure," she says.

We walk out together to the hall, Skye and I turning to face her. We wait until the door to the gym fully closes before we start.

"Just now — you yelled out, 'gay,'" Skye says.

"Yeah," Olivia says.

"Okay, that's not really appropriate," Skye says. "You can't use that language here."

"Why not?" Olivia says, crossing her arms.

"Because it's very harmful," Skye says.

"I didn't mean it like that. I meant it in a fun way. You know," Olivia says, looking at me. "Like we used to joke at school."

She's put me on the spot, but it's too late now. "Yeah," I say, "that wasn't really a joke. That was pretty hurtful."

Olivia stares at me, and she just looks pissed. "You don't get it. *It's not hurtful.* We don't mean it like that."

"Okay, well, we're telling you it is," Skye cuts in. "To the people here, it is. And it's not our job to get you to understand why. But if you're not going to respect that, you need to leave."

"Are you *kidding* me?" Olivia says.

"No," I say. "Skye's right. If you can't understand what's hurtful about your joke, and apologize, then you need to leave."

"You guys are such . . ." Olivia says.

"What? We're such what?" Skye says, cupping her ear.

"You know what? Screw you. Screw you both," Olivia says. "We came here to prove a point, but it's clear that you want to just make us look like bad guys, no matter what we do."

"Nope," Skye says. "That's not true at all. We gave you a chance, we let you play, but you're not being respectful of what this league is all about. So you need to leave."

"*Screw you,*" Olivia says again. She turns and walks back into the gym, Skye and I trailing behind her. For one horrible moment I think Olivia is just going to go back to the game, and we're going to have to actually cause a scene to get her to leave.

But instead, she just walks over to the bench, grabs her water bottle, and heads for the door. She stops on her way out to whisper something to Meaghan.

Meaghan instantly shoots us a dirty look and also goes

over to grab her water bottle. The game has stopped now, everyone watching what's happening. Meaghan motions to Mckenna, Lucy, and Alexis, who all gather around her quickly, and then Meaghan walks off as well.

Slowly, Mckenna and Lucy gather their stuff and follow Meaghan and Olivia out. But Alexis pauses, hesitating on the court.

At the door, Meaghan glances back at Alexis.

"What are you doing?" Meaghan says. "Are you *staying*?"

Alexis hesitates, then slowly nods. She glances over at me and Skye and smiles, hopefully. "If that's okay?" she asks.

I'm stunned, for the second time in the night.

I never thought I'd see her stand up to those girls.

I just nod, slowly, and Skye shrugs.

"Sure, why not?" Skye says. "You didn't say anything."

Alexis smiles. "Thanks."

Meaghan makes a huffing noise, and just like that, the four of them disappear out the gym door. Instantly the whole mood in the gym shifts. I can see people grinning, nudging each other.

But I just want to move past this moment. "Hey! The game clock is still going!" I say, and everyone jumps back into action quickly.

Skye smiles, and gives me a small fist bump before returning to her team's side.

Ms. Arsenault catches me on the other side and gives me a thumbs-up. "Well handled," she says.

"Thanks," I say, smiling.

From then on, the rest of the hour passes in a blur of volleyball: bumping the ball, setting it up for my teammates, rotating positions on court. We don't take it too seriously; we just play. People goof around. We laugh a lot. I have a lot of fun playing, and it's *so* much better because Brooklyn is here, flashing me her gorgeous smile, standing just a few feet away from me on the court.

It's a good night. Ms. Arsenault blows the whistle at 8:05, and reminds us that we've got to get going — there's another group coming to use the gym at 8:30.

We thank everyone for coming, and remind them that it's on next week — same time, same place, bring a friend!

As people head out, Skye and I start taking down the nets. Trevor stays to help us again, and so does Brooklyn, and Alexis.

When it's all done, we all walk out together. Trevor and Ms. Arsenault say goodnight and head off. Alexis gives me and Skye each a hug, tighter than usual, before getting in her dad's car. Brooklyn, Skye, and I linger for a minute on the sidewalk.

"So . . . we slayed," Skye says. "That was pretty intense for a bit, though."

"Yeah," I say. "But I think it went well. I think the social media worked — Skye, you did such a good job with that."

"It was really cool," Brooklyn says. "I'm glad I came."

Skye smiles at her, and raises her eyebrows. "Does that mean you're going to be here next week?"

I'm glad she asked, because I don't think I would have — it would have felt too desperate. But I really want to know.

"Obviously," Brooklyn says. "I'm a part of it now, aren't I?"

"Of course," I say.

"Defs," Skye says. "All right . . . I think my dad's here. I'll see you guys later."

She waves and heads off, leaving me and Brooklyn standing on the sidewalk alone. There's a few cars pulling in and out of the school's parking lot, and some people are heading into the gymnasium — I guess the group who has it after us.

The sun set an hour or so ago, and it's pretty dark now but not completely dark. I can still see Brooklyn's face clearly, her eyes looking at me, her hair in a braid down her back.

"Did you have fun tonight?" I ask her.

She nods. "Oh yeah. That was a lot of fun . . . especially watching you kick the volleyball team out."

I feel myself blushing. "Thanks."

"Is someone coming for you?" she asks, gesturing at the parking lot.

"Yeah, my sister should be here," I say. I glance around the parking lot, scanning for Grace, but I don't see her.

I pull out my phone to check it, and realize I have a missed call from her. At that moment, my phone starts ringing in my hand. Grace is calling me.

"Oh sorry, this is her," I say.

"Oh, right," Brooklyn says. "Okay. Well, I'll see you tomorrow in class?"

"See you tomorrow," I say. She gives me a little wave over her shoulder and heads off. I can see her green car parked across the lot.

I answer the phone. "Hey, what's up?"

"Hey!" Grace says. "Okay, I'm sorry, but I totally spaced and went to a friend's across town and I'm, like, thirty minutes away from being able to pick you up."

"Grace!"

"I know! I'm sorry. Can you get a ride with someone else? Or could Mom or Dad come get you?"

"I don't know, maybe," I say, sighing.

"Okay. Let me know if they can't, and I can come."

"In thirty minutes."

"Yeah. Sorry, I've got to go, but let me know. Love ya!"

She hangs up and I sigh, staring at my phone in my hand. What am I supposed to do now, just stand here and wait for her to come get me? I could try my parents, but I'm pretty sure they're out to dinner with some friends tonight. They might not be able to come get me for thirty minutes, either. I could try calling Skye — she just left a few minutes ago with her dad and they could probably circle back and get me.

Just as I'm trying to decide what to do, Brooklyn pulls up in front of me in her car. Her window is rolled down and she leans out of it, resting an elbow on the window ledge, to talk to me.

"You stuck?" she asks.

"Kind of," I say. "My sister's running super late."

Brooklyn nods. "I could give you a ride home, if you like?"

My heart literally leaps. "You sure? It's out of your way."

"Yeah, no worries," she says, "It's not that far. Hop in."

CHAPTER THIRTEEN

A Ride Home

Brooklyn waits for me to get in and buckle my seat belt before she puts the car in drive.

"I go left from here to get to your house, right?"

"Yeah, left."

The roads are quiet. As we approach Richmond, the light turns red, and Brooklyn starts slowing down.

"Hey," she says, suddenly. "D'you want to get slushies? Like, before I drop you off?"

"Yes," I say, instantly. I don't have to think about it. Yes, I want to.

"Okay," Brooklyn says, grinning. She quickly flicks her blinker on and moves into the left-hand turn lane, into London, instead of the right turn that would lead us to Ilderton.

I don't know if she has a destination in mind, but she drives like she knows where she's going. She has music playing and I just sit and enjoy her songs, watching London go by out the window.

We pass the new builds, and the insane intersection that's Fanshawe and Richmond, and Masonville Mall. We pass a few student residence buildings, and then Brooklyn takes the fork in the road to the right, following it through the university campus. It feels late, but there's still tons of students walking around — some look like they're on their way to class, with backpacks and headphones on, and some are dressed to go out, waiting by the bus stop in groups.

Finally, at the end of the uni buildings, Brooklyn pulls into a parking lot with a 7-Eleven.

"I was starting to wonder where you were taking me," I say as Brooklyn parks. She backs into a spot, making it look easy.

"Don't you trust me?" she asks.

"Mmm . . ." I pretend to think about it as we climb out of the car. She laughs and playfully swats at my arm as we walk into the store.

We walk together to the slushie area, then stand back and survey our options. I keep sneaking glances at Brooklyn. She's in the athletic tank top she played in and has pulled sweatpants on over her shorts. I get distracted just watching her arms and shoulders, the way they move and flow as she leans over to pick up a couple of cups, handing one to me.

"Thanks," I say.

"What flavour are you going to get?" she asks.

"I think Coke."

"Nice. Classic."

"You?"

"Grape, I think."

"Ooh. Also good."

We fill up our cups and head to the front. Brooklyn pays for both of us, and we take them back to the car. Sipping my slushie gives me an instant brain freeze, but the cold and the sugar tastes *so* good after an hour running around on the court.

I figured we'd start heading back now, but to my surprise, Brooklyn drives across the street and heads into campus.

At the first parking lot, Brooklyn swings right. I've been on campus a handful of times for school trips, and once for an official campus tour with Noah when he was deciding where he wanted to go for uni. I recognize the football stadium at the end of the parking lot we're in now.

Brooklyn parks near the front, facing the trees, and looks at me. "Want to go drink these by the river?"

"Yes," I say.

My god, I think I love her.

I follow her across the grass and to a break in the trees. It's not as dark out here as I thought it would be, and we find a spot to sit on a large rock beside the river. The water is gliding smoothly below us. A little farther down the river we can see the bridge, with a steady flow of traffic — cars, bikes, and walkers — on it.

We sit side by side on the rock, sipping our slushies. I rest my other hand on the rock between us; Brooklyn's hand is close to my own.

"This is a good spot," I say. "You come here a lot?"

"Not a ton," Brooklyn says. "Usually in the summer. Campus is quieter then."

"You know, I like it more with all the people," I say. "It's got . . . I dunno . . . nice energy or something."

"Yeah," Brooklyn says. "It's cool in the summer, though. It feels like you have the whole place to yourselves, almost."

"Do you normally . . . uh . . . come out here alone, or with people?"

"Oh, I bring all my dates here," Brooklyn says. She catches sight of my face and laughs. "No, I'm kidding. I mean, I don't bring all of my dates here. I mean . . . I usually come out here with my friends."

"Oh," I say. "Okay."

My mind is frantically trying to run through what she just said. Is she trying to say that we're on a date? Or is she trying to say that we're *not* on a date?

"It's a nice spot to sit and think, too," Brooklyn says. "It's really basic, but I like seeing the buildings and thinking about what it'll be like when I'm in uni."

"That's not basic," I say. "I think that's just visualization."

"I'm manifesting," Brooklyn says, and we laugh.

"Do you know where you want to go?" I ask her.

"Not sure," she says. "I don't know if I want to go to a party school like Western, or somewhere more chill. I'd like to try a break from small towns, though. I love them, but I'd like to try living *in* a city, not just on the edges. Somewhere with a little more action, you know? More stuff going on."

"I get that," I say. "I really get that. Do you . . . do you go to a lot of queer events?"

"Not a ton, to be honest," Brooklyn says. "Cause like . . . I know that things have changed a lot, and it should be fine to be queer, but it's still kind of weird to be out in high school. Almost like . . . you're more popular than you should be? Do you know what I mean?"

"No," I tell her, honestly, and it makes her laugh. "Brooklyn, I think you're just popular."

"No!" she says, laughing. "No, I mean, like . . . okay, like this summer, a bunch of my friends wanted to go to Pride in Toronto. All my straight friends. They were really excited about it, and they kept saying that it was 'my day,' but it felt like I was just their excuse to go. Like they were waiting to have a gay friend so that they could go to Pride."

"That's insane," I say. "Straight people are crazy sometimes. Did you have fun, at least?"

"No!" Brooklyn says. "We watched the parade for, like, twenty minutes, and then they realized that the parade lasts for four hours, and they didn't want to watch the whole thing. So they made me leave so that we could go get food somewhere, but obviously all of the places in the area were packed, and most places wouldn't have even let us in, anyway, because we were underage. So we ended up having to walk, like, thirty minutes to eat. And it was a million degrees in Toronto, so we were all too hot and grumpy by the end."

"Sucks," I say. "I can't believe they would do that, on *your* special day!"

I'm being sarcastic, and she laughs. Every time I make her laugh, I feel this insane glow of happiness.

"I didn't even want to go!" she says. "I would have been happy just watching the London Pride parade. Close to home. Easy."

"Next time," I say. "You'll know better."

"Yeah. Or I'll just get wasted. I've heard that makes it a lot better," Brooklyn says. "What about you? Have you ever been to Pride?"

"No," I say. "I'd like to go, but . . . I dunno, I feel kind of weird going right now. I'm still figuring out that part of my identity, I guess. Like, I know I'm queer, but I don't know how I want to . . . present it? If that makes sense. I'm afraid of just becoming a stereotype."

"Right," Brooklyn says, joking. "You mean like wearing Converse, the backwards baseball hats, playing on a women's basketball team . . ."

She's just describing herself, and I burst out laughing.

"Yes," I say. "Exactly. But no — like, I'm just afraid of doing something, or dressing a certain way, and then putting myself in a box."

"Okay, that makes sense," Brooklyn says. "And yet, you started an inclusive volleyball league."

"Yeah," I say, and I shrug. "I guess that's where I'm at. Like, I'm not wearing rainbow stuff, but I'd go to a drag brunch."

"I'd go to a drag brunch with you," Brooklyn says.

"Yeah?"

Okay. That's a date. Right? That's got to be a date.

Unless it's just, like, queer friendship. Maybe she just wants more queer friends.

"Yeah," she says.

On the rock, Brooklyn moves her hand over so that the sides of our hands are pressed together. I suddenly realize that we've been moving closer and closer together, leaning in, as we talk.

"You're, like, really pretty," I say.

"You are too," she says.

I'm not sure who closes the small gap between us — if she leans the last bit in, or if I do — all I know is that in a split second, it's gone, and we're kissing. Our hands in each other's hair, her mouth on mine, and completely wrapped up in each other, on this warm rock by the river.

* * *

A while later, Brooklyn drives us back. It's even more impossible not to stare at her now as she drives — the way she glances around before each intersection, the way the streetlights hit her face as we drive, throwing her in and out of light. She's so beautiful.

It feels surreal, that we just kissed by the river.

At red lights, she reaches over and holds my hand on top of the gear shift, her thumb gently running along the side of my hand.

We talk the whole way back, and our conversation flows so easily.

"How long have you had your license?" I ask. I want to know everything about her.

"Two months," she says. "It's so nice, not having to ask my parents for a ride everywhere. Are you driving yet?"

"I'm working on it," I say. "I'm studying for my G1."

Brooklyn lets go of my hand to take a drink of her slushie. I've finished mine already. She holds her cup out to me.

"Want a sip?" she asks.

"Thanks," I say.

We just made out, and yet I'm still excited to put my lips where hers just were.

When we get into Ilderton, she remembers the way to my house, even though she's only been there once before. She pulls up to the curb in front of my house and turns off her car. We sit in the darkness, neither of us moving. I don't want to get out of the car. Tonight has been so special, I'm suddenly afraid of it ending.

"Hey, Mackenzie?" Brooklyn says.

"Yeah?"

"Um . . . I was thinking, if you're interested . . . would you want to go out sometime?"

Oh my god, oh my god . . .

"This could be, like, our unofficial first date, but . . . I'd love to plan something with you," Brooklyn says. She looks at me and I realize she's kind of nervous, asking me, and it makes my heart feel all kinds of ways. Does she think there's any universe in which I'd say no?

"Okay," I say, smiling.

"Yeah?"

"Yeah, I'd really like that. But I'd like to plan it, if you're game, since you took us around tonight."

Brooklyn smiles back. "Okay," she says. "I trust you."

Slowly, we move closer and we kiss again.

Kissing her makes every part of me feel on fire. I've never felt anything like this before.

Finally, we move apart.

"Goodnight," I say.

"Night," she says.

I climb out of the car and walk up the driveway to my house slowly, wanting to savour the last few moments of the night. I hear Brooklyn start her car and drive away, slowly. I wonder if she's wanting to hang on to the last few moments of tonight, too.

Smiling, I go inside. I've just had, hands down, the best night of my life.

CHAPTER FOURTEEN

Team Found

Four weeks later, I'm sitting in the kitchen, waiting for my ride to get here. It's Thursday night and tonight is the sixth week of the inclusive volleyball league.

Amazingly, people have continued to show up each week. Trevor hasn't missed a week. Grace came for the first time last week, and Alexis has been a regular. We have a few regular people showing up each night, too . . . including Brooklyn. It's nice having her there and also a complete distraction, watching her play.

We also, surprisingly, had two of the volleyball girls come back: Mckenna and Lucy. They apologized for what Olivia had said, and for seeing some of the other stuff that had happened when I was on the team and never saying anything about it.

They seemed really genuine with their apology — I just wished they'd been able to say some of it the week before, in front of Meaghan and Olivia. I felt torn, once again, about letting them play or not. But in the end, Skye and I decided that we should give them another chance. I still don't know if the volleyball co-captains know that they're coming, or they're showing up in secret. But they're showing up, anyway, and they've been told that any more bad ally behaviour, and they're out.

And the league has stayed fun. Games are good, nobody takes it too seriously, and we've started doing stretches together in a big circle before each game, which is weirdly bonding. We've had enough people to play four vs. four each week, sometimes with subs, sometimes without. I'm hopeful that we'll get eight people again tonight.

My phone buzzes with a text from Brooklyn: *here!*

My heart leaping, I get up and head outside.

Brooklyn is waiting for me at the curb. She's been picking me up and giving me a ride to the league every week, ever since the night of our slushies. It still feels surreal that she's here for me. This girl that I rate higher than anyone is here for *me*.

We've had five dates over the last month — basically any time we can find free between school, her basketball practices, and family stuff.

For our first date I took her to the Ilderton Fall Fair. We

walked around the ag barns and saw prize-winning corn, cows, and quilts; we shared a funnel cake; we watched the parade. We decided to take our chances on a couple of the rides and rode on a *very* sketchy scrambler-style ride that sounded like all the nails in it were rattling loose as we were in midair. We spent an hour standing in line for the Ferris wheel, just so that we could kiss at the top. It felt like we were in *Happiest Season*, but an autumn gays edition.

We've taken turns planning dates since then. Brooklyn took me to the drive-in theatre south of London; I took her to the world's worst minigolf course; she took me to the arcade and obstacle course at 100 Kellogg; I took her to Saga, the board game café.

She's planning something for us this Saturday. I can't wait. No matter what it is, though, I'm sure I'll have fun — I just like spending time with her.

"Hey," Brooklyn says when I get in the car.

"Hey," I say, smiling at her. I slide over and we kiss for a minute.

"You ready?" she asks and I nod.

"Let's go!"

We're halfway there, chatting and holding hands whenever we can, when Skye calls me. That's weird. We never call each other.

"Hey," I say, answering my phone.

"Hey," Skye says. She sounds a little out of breath. "Are you on your way?"

"Yeah, we're five minutes away. I'm with Brooklyn."

"Okay, hurry," Skye says.

"What's wrong? Is everything okay?"

"Just . . . you'll see when you get here," Skye says and hangs up.

Brooklyn glances over. "What's up?" she asks.

"I don't know," I say. "She didn't say."

I'm panicking. Something must be wrong — maybe she can't get into the gym? Or the nets are missing?

Or . . . maybe it's something worse. Is there going to be a group of protestors or something outside the gym? Could it be those angry parents that Mr. Stapleton was so worried about? I bite my lip, looking out the window, and Brooklyn squeezes my hand.

The last part of the drive seems to take forever, even though I know it's only a few minutes, and I'm pretty sure Brooklyn is speeding a little to make it even faster.

Finally, we pull into the parking lot, and my heart sinks. *No.* There's a crowd waiting around the gym doors. It's a little dark out and hard to completely see who they are, but there's definitely a crowd there. Not a ton of people, but maybe eight or ten of them.

Brooklyn parks and we sit in the car, staring at the crowd. I don't know what to do. Is Skye inside? Should I push through the people to get through? What are they going to do?

Slowly, we get out of the car and stand beside it, still a safe distance away.

"Hey," Brooklyn says, squinting. "Do those look like . . . How old are they?"

Just then, I see Skye, pushing her way out through the crowd. She's spotted us and jogs over, waving frantically.

"What are you *doing*?" she says. "Come on — get in here already!"

"What — through there?" I say alarmed, gesturing at the crowd.

"Yeah, they'll move for us," Skye says.

"But . . . aren't they protesting?" I ask.

At the same time, Brooklyn says, suddenly, "Mackenzie, I think they're teenagers."

Skye stares at me, her eyes bugging out. "*Protesting*? No, dummy, they're here for the league! I've been holding them at bay as long as I can, but they really want to come in. Come on, get in here, help me set up the nets so we can let them in!"

"But . . . how . . ."

Skye takes my arm and starts dragging me towards the gym. Brooklyn jogs to catch up and follows closely behind.

When we get to the crowd, I realize that Brooklyn is right — they're all teenagers. As we push through, people start asking Skye how long it will be until they can go in.

"Soon, soon!" she says, impatiently swatting them away. "Let us in so we can set up the nets already!"

There's definitely an energy in the crowd, but it's not the angry mob that I imagined here to protest our inclusive sports league.

People are chatting with each other, laughing, jumping up and down and stretching. They're *excited.*

And, suddenly, so am I.

We hustle into the gym and quickly start helping Skye set up the nets. It takes two people to set up each net, so we work together, chatting excitedly as we go.

"How long have they been there?" I ask Skye.

"Like, fifteen minutes," Skye says. "A couple of them were already here when *I* got here. I asked if they knew it didn't start 'til seven, and they said they did — they were just really excited and wanted to come early."

"That's insane," I say. "I can't believe it."

I'm half afraid that they're all going to get bored out there and leave.

"It looks like the word's finally gotten out," Brooklyn says. "Must have been the posters."

"Or the social media posts," I say.

"Or people told their friends," Skye suggests.

Ms. Arsenault arrives a few minutes later. She walks in the door looking stunned.

"Did you see all the people out there?" she exclaims.

"Yeah, we did," I say, grinning.

"It's amazing," Ms. Arsenault says. "This is so exciting. It makes me so hopeful for the future, to see all those kids out there, ready to join this league . . ."

"Right," Skye says. "Very excited for the future. Hey, could you help us set up the last net? Then we can actually let them in . . ."

As soon as the nets are up, Skye opens the doors. There's even more people now; I count fifteen, then twenty, then twenty-five. Brooklyn and I pass off volleyballs for people to warm up with, but we run out quickly. As new people arrive, we instruct them to join previous pairs who are warming up. Everyone is super friendly and welcoming to each new person who walks in.

Soon, people are practicing in large groups across the gym. Volleyballs are flying everywhere, and the gym is full of the sounds of people laughing and talking.

For a moment, I stand there, drinking it all in and listening to the conversations happening all around me:

"Here!"

"Got it!"

"Hi! You can join our group!"

"Got it!"

"I'm so bad at this, ha!"

"Do we get team names?"

"Here!"

"Hey, I *love* your shirt!"

"Hi! What's your name?"

"Nice one!"

"I'm Marco."

"Hey! Come on, there's room in our group!"

"Nice to meet you!"

"Wait, I've got it — I got it! I did it! I hit the ball!"

"Amazing!"

"Good one!"

People keep coming in. We wait until ten past seven, and then Ms. Arsenault suggests we should get started. By my count, there's about forty teens here now.

Ms. Arsenault, Skye, and I stand in a huddle, discussing how to do this.

"I can call everyone's attention," Ms. Arsenault says, "And then you two could organize people into teams?"

"For sure," Skye says. "We can do that."

"And maybe, before we split everyone off, one of you would like to say a few words to welcome people here? Maybe you could restate what the league is all about, and thank them for coming?"

Skye looks over at me. "I think you should do it, Kenzie. This is your thing."

"This is *our* thing," I correct her.

"Yeah, but it was your idea," Skye says. "You should do it."

"Er . . . okay," I say reluctantly. I'm kind of afraid of speaking to the crowd, but it looks like there's no turning back.

"Okay," Ms. Arsenault says, her eyes twinkling.

We break our huddle and move so that we're standing in a line, facing the rest of the gym together. Ms. Arsenault raises her hands and claps a pattern, the way that teachers do to call your attention. Instantly, forty pairs of hands drop what they're doing and clap the pattern back. Silence falls over the gym, aside from the noise of a few wayward volleyballs bouncing away, and a few muttered, "*Oops*!"

"Good evening!" Ms. Arsenault says. "My name is Katie Arsenault. I'm a teacher at Medway High, and the chaperone a.k.a. supervisor of this league. Beside me are Mackenzie and Skye, the league's co-founders. We're going to get started in just a minute here, but first, Mackenzie has a quick word for you all."

She gestures to me and I take a small step forward. Suddenly, everybody's eyes are on me. I feel myself sweating.

The entire gym is staring at me; what am I supposed to say to them? Oh yeah — thank them for coming out.

"Thanks," I say, and my voice breaks a little. I flush and clear my throat, then raise my voice so it's a little louder, stronger this time. "Thank you, everyone, for coming out tonight. It really, uh . . . it means a lot to us to see you all here."

My mind is blanking. *What am I supposed to say?* They're all looking at me.

Desperately, I scan the crowd. I see Trevor, who grins and gives me a thumbs up. And then I see Brooklyn, standing not too far away, and she gives me an excited smile.

There's something about her face, the way her eyes are locked on mine. She gives me an encouraging nod, and it's like she's saying, *You got this!*

It feels like she's right beside me, and I feel better. My heart calming a bit, I take a deep breath.

Restate what the league is all about. That's what Ms. Arsenault suggested. I can do that.

"This league is open for any teen in the area — whether that's, you know, London or Arva or Ilderton or Thorndale — so long as you agree with the league's mandate," I say, "which is being a fun and safe place for 2SLGBTQIA+ teens and allies to make friends, play volleyball, and build community."

Skye and I wrote the mandate weeks ago, with Ms. Arsenault's help. I didn't really understand what "build community" meant, but we added it at Ms. Arsenault's suggestion. Looking around the gym, at all the people who I've just watched meet for the first time and happily start chatting, I think I might get it now.

"So . . . that's it," I say. "It's really great to see you all, and I hope you have fun and come back next week, too. We're here every week. And it's okay if you suck at volleyball! It's just about being here . . . with each other . . . and having a good time."

Ms. Arsenault tucks her water bottle under her arm and starts clapping for me. For a split second, I'm absolutely mortified — oh my god, how embarrassing is it to have an adult slow-clapping for you in front of everyone — but Skye and Brooklyn quickly join in, and so does Trevor, and then so does everyone.

It only lasts a minute, but my cheeks turn pink. And I feel warm from head to toe. Because all these people, they showed up tonight for a league where everyone could feel safe. And I know it's not just about me, and that they showed up for each other, too, but it also kinda feels like they showed up for me.

"Okay!" I say once the applause dies down. "Um . . .

cool. Well, let's get organized into teams then. I think we can actually get four games going, with alternates . . . so let's do it this way — if you've played volleyball before, move to that side of the gym, and if you've never played before, move to *that* side of the gym, and then we can split everyone up so that there's an equal amount of playing experience on each team . . ."

People start moving, and to my surprise, there's only about fifteen people who have played before. Everyone else is standing on the other side.

Skye and I split, with each of us taking a side, and we number people off — *one, two, three, four, five, six, seven, eight* — and then Skye stands up on a bench and gives people a quick reminder of the rules of the game.

"That's it!" she says, wrapping up. "Remember to sub in your alternates, and don't take it too seriously! Okay, this court will be team one vs. team two — and team three vs. team four there — this one is for team five vs. team six — and team seven vs. team eight, you're over here!"

It's chaos — pure, wonderful chaos. Ms. Arsenault doesn't have to play anymore. She sits on a bench in the centre and just watches everything going on happily and cheering for random teams. Skye and I don't play, either, we just walk around all night, helping organize and answering people's questions. They have a lot of them.

"Where's the washroom?"

"Is this out of bounds?"

"Am I allowed to catch the ball?"

"How do you spike it?"

"Is there anywhere to fill up water?"

"Is the league on TikTok?"

"Can you take our photo?"

"Is that out of bounds?"

"Can you take our photo with everyone?"

"Can we tag you in this?"

"Is the washroom down this hall?"

I see people chatting happily on the sidelines as they wait for their turn to play, and I watch people high-five each other in between sets. One team — all made up of people who have met for the first time tonight — keeps making jokes and can't stop laughing on the court. At the end of their set, they ask me to take their photo in front of the net, and they all stand close together, arms wrapped around each other's shoulders, grinning ear-to-ear.

Brooklyn's been sorted into team five; I find a lot of excuses to wander over near that court. When she's on the sidelines at one point, waiting to sub back in, I walk over and stand next to her.

"This is amazing, Mackenzie," she says. She leans against

me. She's warm from playing, and I can feel the heat from her body radiating into mine.

"Thanks," I say, smiling.

"Sub in!" one of her teammates calls.

"Gotta go," she says. She squeezes my hand and then jogs onto court. Another girl, who was standing on my other side, waiting for her turn to sub back in for team seven, leans over to me.

"Are you two dating?" she whispers, excited.

I nod, feeling a secret thrill. "Yeah," I whisper back.

"Oh my god!" she says. "You two make *such* a cute couple. Did you meet through the league?"

"Thanks!" I say, smiling. "I guess . . . we sort of did."

"That's so sweet, oh my god, couple goals," she says. Just then, someone from her team jogs off court — she's in. "Oh, gotta go!"

I move on, walking around the gym and answering more questions, but the smile doesn't leave my face for the rest of the night.

The hour passes in a rush, and all too quickly, it comes to an end. Ms. Arsenault blows a whistle at ten past eight — when did she get a whistle? — and tells people it's time to head home.

"Thank you for coming, but our time slot is almost over!"

Ms. Arsenault says. "Don't forget to take all your water bottles and bags . . . and come back next week!"

Skye, Brooklyn, Trevor, and I start taking down the nets. We keep getting interrupted by people coming up to thank us for organizing everything.

It takes people forever to leave — they linger, chatting in large groups, some people standing and some sitting on the floor.

Finally, once we have the nets and equipment all put away, Ms. Arsenault tells people again that it's time to go.

"Come on, we'll see you next week!" she says, gently shooing people out.

Outside, people are still standing, chatting and laughing. Nobody is in a rush to go anywhere. Ms. Arsenault waits until we're all out of the gym, and then shrugs.

"That'll do, I guess," she says. "Goodnight, Mackenzie, Skye, Trevor! Goodnight, everyone!"

She waves and we all wave back, watching her head off.

Skye, Brooklyn, Trevor, and I stand in a small group together, watching the crowds of people still standing here, talking.

"This was incredible," Skye says. "I can't believe how many people showed up."

"It's probably a one-off," I say. "We got really lucky, or

everyone decided to come out to try it once tonight. Next week we may be back to just eight or so people."

"Nah," Skye says. "I have a good feeling about this."

"I think a lot of them will come back," Trevor says. "People were having a great time playing. And a lot of them got so much better through the night."

"Yeah, that was really fun," Brooklyn says. She's standing beside me and notices the goosebumps on my arms — it was so warm in the gym with all the people in there and there's a slight chill in the air out here. "Are you cold?"

"A bit," I say.

Brooklyn reaches into her gym bag and pulls out a spare hoodie, which she hands to me. "Here."

I pull on Brooklyn's hoodie, feeling instantly warmer. It smells like her, like turmeric and honey. I put my hands in the pockets and huddle down inside of it, inhaling.

Skye, watching us, smirks. "You guys are, like, stupid cute."

"How long have you been dating?" Trevor asks.

"Like, a month?" Brooklyn says, glancing at me for confirmation. I nod. "A month."

"Hey!"

We look up to see one of the teens from a group that's standing near us walking over. I think his name might be Marco.

"Hey!" Skye says. "What's up?"

"A bunch of us are going out for pizza," Marco says. "Do you guys want to come? You're all invited."

He looks around at us, his face open, kind, and welcoming. I glance at the group behind him and see that they're waiting for us, all of them smiling.

Skye smiles. "Sure. I have time."

Trevor nods, too. "Yeah, for sure!"

Brooklyn glances at me. "You wanna go?"

I nod. Taking one of my hands out of the hoodie pocket, I slide it into Brooklyn's hand. "Yeah. That sounds fun. Let's do it."

"Great," Marco says. "We're meeting at King Richie's — does anyone need a ride?"

"I can take us four," Brooklyn says. "We have room for one more, too, if anyone needs it?"

"Sure, thanks! You can follow us. We're going to convoy . . ."

We walk with the group, everyone chatting and laughing, to the cars in the parking lot. There, we all start squeezing into the four or so cars that people have.

"Shotgun!" Skye says, as we walk over.

Brooklyn rolls her eyes and points to me. "Nice try. Shotgun is reserved."

Brooklyn's car is filled with me, Skye, Trevor, and a person named Elle. I sit in the passenger seat, feeling insanely special. Our giant group waits until everyone's in a car, ensuring that nobody gets left behind, before we start off. Driving in a little convoy together, we head down Richmond Street. At each stop light, Brooklyn reaches over and takes my hand, like usual, neither of us caring that there's other people in the car to see our PDA.

I put on some music as we drive. Skye, Trevor, and Elle are chatting away in the back seat, already acting as if they've all known each other forever. It feels good to see everyone hanging out and making new friends. And it feels so good to be included with them.

But even better than that — and definitely the best part of it all, by far — is the feeling of Brooklyn's hand in mine as we go.

Acknowledgements

Thank you to Allister Thompson and the Lorimer team for your work on this project.

Thank you to the Ontario Arts Council, who gave me the Recommender grant that connected me with the Lorimer team.

Thank you to Kyla, for letting us start the FCSSC LGBTQ2+ curling league and trusting me with it. Thank you to the community member who first brought the idea to us, and to all the people who signed up for the league — and who continue to sign up.

The statistics listed by Mackenzie in Chapter 3 are real, and are based on results from Out on the Fields (2015) and OutSport (2019), international research on homophobia and transphobia in sport. For more information see: outonthefields.com.

Joyfully, all of the 2SLGBTQIA+ sport organizations that Mackenzie learns about in Chapter 3 are also real and active at the time of writing. Thank you to all of the people, within these organizations or elsewhere, working to make accessible, inclusive, fun spaces for sport. Thank you to my family and friends who sent messages of support, added the book to their carts, and told me they couldn't wait to read it.

Finally, thank you to Maddie, for your encouragement that I take on this project and for giving me the space to write.